PRAISE FOR *THE*

"Each character is more ch[...] the intellectual discussions [...] fresh and engaging and will keep the pages turning. A quick-witted depiction of moviemaking best suited for contemplative romantics."

—*Kirkus Reviews*

"*The Location Shoot*, penned by Patricia Leavy, is an enlightening exploration of art, philosophy, and life's profound queries. . . . The narrative's charm isn't solely defined by the romantic entanglement of a central couple but also by its well-sketched ensemble cast . . . the story reaches a fulfilling conclusion, brimming with a sense of humanity and personal transformation."

—Literary Titan, 5-star review

"A tour de force! Much more than a romance, this novel celebrates the romance of life itself. Set on an exotic film location with a fabulous cast of characters that comes to life on the page, this book grabs hold of your heart and mind. *The Location Shoot* poses big questions about the meaning of life and love, and the answers are profoundly satisfying. Leavy's voice in fiction is singular. She brings her laser-like wit, intelligence, and hopefulness to this enchanting and truly unforgettable love story."

—Laurel Richardson, author of *Lone Twin*

"*The Location Shoot* is a stunning exploration of love, hope, dreams, and art bundled together in sheets of romance and laughter overheard from characters you just want to spend more and more time with. A truly joyous read!"

—J. E. Sumerau, author of *Scarecrow*

"*The Location Shoot* by Patricia Leavy is a fun and light summer escape for romance fans. A perfect book to take to the pool."
— Sarahlyn Bruck, author of *Light of the Fire*

"*The Location Shoot* is a masterpiece. Leavy's astonishing talent for exploring the human condition through light and escapist reading is on full display in this gorgeously written novel. Sexy celebrity romance meets rom-com meets literary fiction. This profoundly engaging book gave me all the feelings, from laughter to happy tears. I fell completely in love with the characters through Leavy's masterful dialogue. This book was so captivating that I read it in one sitting, unable to put it down. The ending is pure perfection."
—U. Melissa Anyiwo, editor of *Gender Warriors*

"An intelligent, thought-provoking romance set in a gorgeous location in the endlessly riveting world of filmmaking. *The Location Shoot* is absolutely spellbinding. The atmospheric details are exquisite, the characters finely drawn, and the story captivating. This book is a celebration of love, friendship, and the magic of art. Completely immersive; I could not put it down! The ending is unforgettable and deeply satisfying. A must-read!"
—Jessica Smartt Gullion, author of *October Birds*

"Wow! Leavy has written a gorgeous novel about the meaning of life and how art is woven into the fabric of human existence. The characters show us that the biggest question is best answered through art and love. Life, like art, is about improvisation, taking chances, and pushing through our fear. I devoured this book."
—Sandra L. Faulkner, author of *Poetic Inquiry: Craft, Method and Practice*

"Leavy's latest novel is less about the film world as a place of make believe and more about the real questions of life. Get the book, get on location, enjoy!"
—Mary E. Weems, Cleveland Arts Prize winner and author of *Blackeyed*

"Quaint romance gives way to a deeper allegory about human development. Leavy illustrates how a lifetime of intense publicity and relentless exposure can trap people in an eternal childhood of the heart, from which they must break free. I expect—and hope—to see Finn Forrester and Ella Sinclair in the news again."
—Alexandra "Xan" Nowakowski, coauthor of *Other People's Oysters*

"Life imitates art in this wildly romantic novel. Leavy's unique talent for weaving a thoughtful meditation on the arts into a sexy beach read is on full display in this triumphant page-turner of a book that follows the personal lives of a group making a film about the meaning of life. You will fall in love with the characters, but more than anything, *The Location Shoot* makes you fall in love with life itself. A profoundly beautiful and inspiring read. I didn't want it to end. Highly recommend!"
—Jessie Voigts, PhD, founder of Wandering Educators

PRAISE FOR
PATRICIA LEAVY'S *HOLLYLAND*

"This quick read will leave readers satisfied with the happy ending. The main characters will make readers believe in love. Fans of Colleen Hoover and Tessa Bailey will enjoy *Hollyland*."
—*Booklist*

"Some fun secondary characters, a well-drawn setting, and an exciting eleventh-hour kidnapping plot propel Leavy's story. The author also offers rich details about Rye's Hollywood world and Dee's opinions on art . . ."
—*Kirkus Reviews*

". . . Leavy weaves a lot of excitement, charm, and romance into this concise and highly engrossing novel . . . the action really ramps up in the latter section of the book to offer a superb climax filled with suspense. Overall, I would not hesitate to recommend *Hollyland* to fans of romance and women's fiction everywhere; you will not be disappointed."
—*Readers' Favorite*, 5-star review

"Written with the kind of eloquence associated with award winning literary fiction . . . An impressively poignant, laudably original, and thoroughly entertaining novel that moves fluidly between romance, humor, suspense, and joy, *Hollyland* is one of those stories that will linger in the mind and memory long after the book itself has been finished and set back upon the shelf . . . highly recommended."
—*Midwest Book Review*

THE LOCATION SHOOT

THE
LOCATION
SHOOT

a novel

PATRICIA LEAVY

SHE WRITES PRESS

Published 2023
Printed in the United States of America
Print ISBN: 978-1-64742-567-8
E-ISBN: 978-1-64742-568-5
Library of Congress Control Number: 2023907852

For information, address:
She Writes Press
1569 Solano Ave #546
Berkeley, CA 94707

Interior Design by Tabitha Lahr

She Writes Press is a division of SparkPoint Studio, LLC.

For Mark Robins

PROLOGUE

June 30   *Entertainment News Report*

On the heels of his costly third divorce, controversial French filmmaker Jean Mercier has announced the cast for his highly anticipated new English-language film. Shooting starts tomorrow at a secret location in Sweden. Mercier, 58, famously films in remote locations, living in seclusion with his lead actors in rented homes and inns. The award winner is known for his unconventional, avant-garde approach to filmmaking, and for curating unexpected casts. He's certainly done it again.

Leading the cast is acclaimed British actor of stage and screen Albie Hughes, 73, who is teaming up once again with the tempestuous director, perhaps hoping to score another Oscar for his collection. British actress Charlotte Reed, 40, is also set to star in the film. Reed is best known for her dramatic work, often appearing on stage at London's West End theaters, although she has recently become a staple in the independent film scene.

Hollywood film star Finn Forrester, 42, who began his career as a teen heartthrob before growing into a formidable presence on the silver screen, has appeared in over one hundred feature films. The Mercier project is a departure for the legendary actor, who in recent years has been cashing in as the star of blockbuster action-adventure movies. American actor Michael Hennesey, 38, best known for his Emmy-winning role on *Desperation and Despair*, is also set to star in the unnamed film. Perhaps most surprising, American actress Willow Barnes, 28, rounds out the cast. Barnes began her career as a tween star, which she parlayed into a short-lived turn as a pop singer and scream queen. After a series of highly publicized, drunken escapades, several failed celebrity relationships, four DUI charges, and two stints in rehab, Barnes has not performed in over three years, although she remains one of the most followed celebrities on social media.

Mercier remains tight-lipped on the details of the film and his surprising casting choices. One thing is for sure: if it's anything like his other pictures, it's going to be a daring work of cinema that pushes the performers and audiences past their comfort zones. The film is scheduled to shoot for three months.

 **CHAPTER 1**

"You should hear what she wrote about ménage à trois! Her section on the logistics of how it all works blew my mind. I thought that we French were the ones open about matters of the flesh, but we have nothing on our dear American friend, Ms. Ella Sinclair," Luc said.

Everyone broke out into hearty laughter, causing other patrons in the bistro to glance over at the rambunctious group.

Simone traipsed in and dropped a newspaper on the table. "You'll have to fill me in on what's so funny. Sorry I'm late. I hope you ordered for me." Luc nodded and Simone continued, "I stopped at a newsstand and flipped the paper open to the entertainment section to see if there was a mention of my upcoming gallery exhibit, but I got sidetracked. There's a big story about Jean Mercier's upcoming film shoot. You all know what a fan of his I am. Ella, I still can't believe you're friends with him. He's an extraordinary artist, an icon, a national treasure."

Ella smiled. "We go way back. He certainly has quite a big personality."

"So, we shouldn't believe all the stories about what a lecher he is?" Luc asked.

"Well, I wouldn't go that far, but he's a dear friend and a brilliant artist," Ella replied.

"Fill me in on what was so funny," Simone said.

"We were talking about Ella's latest manuscript. I'm telling you, I was glad to be home alone reading it. How can I say this? It was quite, uh . . . sensual," Luc replied.

Ella playfully rolled her eyes. "It's a philosophical treatise on sex, not erotica."

"It's a multifunctional text," Luc said. "The best ones always are."

Ella giggled.

The waiter delivered their drinks and scrumptious food.

"Ah, saved by alcohol," Ella said.

Everyone raised their glasses. "*À votre santé!*"

"Mmm, this place has the most sublime Bellinis," Ella remarked, taking a sip.

"They use white peaches this time of year," Luc explained.

"Figures. Everything is better in Paris, even brunch," Ella said, pulling her long, light brown spirals into a loose bun at the nape of her neck.

"I can't disagree with that," Clara said, biting into her buttery brioche. "So, what does our American girl in Paris have planned for the summer? I was thinking we could all take a trip to the south. We need a holiday. Let's sunbathe on La Côte d'Azur and gorge ourselves on fresh seafood."

"I'm free after my gallery opening," Simone said.

"Ooh, I'm in," another added.

"Me too," someone else chimed in.

"Ella?" Luc asked.

"Sounds divine, but I'm not sure. Jean's film is shooting somewhere in the Swedish countryside over the next three months. He's invited me to tag along. Knowing him, he'll pester me until I agree. I haven't committed to anything yet, but I'll probably go at some point. The change of scenery might do my writing some good."

"Who says no to being on the set of a Jean Mercier film, in picturesque Sweden, no less?" Simone said.

Ella smiled. "Visiting his location shoots is always a treat. One never knows what will happen. Plus, it's a chance for some quiet time. I could use a break from the city." She took a bite of her *oeufs en cocotte* and said, "But I would miss this, the company and the heavenly food."

"Go to Sweden, darling. It's a once-in-a-lifetime experience," Simone said. "But wait until after my show. I don't want you to miss it."

"Of course, if you want to meet a beautiful man and have a steamy affair, come to the Riviera with us. This is what the French do best, after all, especially in the summertime. You're too gorgeous and fabulous to be alone. Romance beckons. You can always call it research and development for your next book," Luc said.

Ella giggled. "The last thing I'm looking for is a man."

"Then watch out," Luc cautioned. "That's one thing we French seem to understand better than you Americans: lightning always strikes when we least expect it."

"ALBIE, DARLING, WOULD YOU LIKE more tea?" Margaret asked, placing the hand-painted porcelain pot on the coffee table.

He shook his head and reached out for her hand. "Sit down with me, my love."

She sat beside him on the couch, and he draped his arm around her. "Let's just be still together until I have to go," he said.

"When is the car service picking you up?" she asked, nuzzling closer to him.

"About an hour. They're getting Charlotte first. I thought it would be nice for us to travel together since she's so nearby. It will give us a chance to catch up."

"When was the last time you worked together?" Margaret asked.

"About four years ago, when we did that show at the National Theatre."

"Ah, how could I forget? Your performance was so lovely."

He kissed the side of her head. "I know you'd prefer if I stayed with you this summer."

"I'll just be wandering around this old townhouse like a loose marble in an empty drawer."

"Margaret . . ."

"Don't worry. London will keep me busy, always does. I'll work on the garden, volunteer at the library, see my friends. It's just that you fill this space so perfectly. It's a bit lonely without you, that's all."

"It's difficult to be away from you too. I hope you know that."

"There's no need for us to be maudlin," she interrupted. "You must work. After all these years, I understand that. It's just . . . I worry about you, darling. You never say a word about it, but I know you haven't been feeling well. What if . . ."

He squeezed her. "My sweet Margaret, please don't worry. I'm stronger than you think. Like an ox. This will be good for me."

"Promise me you'll take care of yourself."

"I will."

"When you come home . . ."

"We'll spend every moment together. I'm sure I'll drive you batshit mad. You won't be able to get rid of me," he said.

She smiled and rested her head on his shoulder.

He sighed. "But oh, how I will miss you, my love."

"CAN'T WE AT LEAST DISCUSS IT?" Charlotte asked.

"The car is picking you up soon. This really isn't the time. Besides, I must get down to the theater. Yesterday's auditions were an absolute disaster. Bloody hell, it's like they've never heard of Shakespeare. It's so much easier when I can just cast you. You are the most brilliant actress."

She feigned a smile.

"I really ought to go," he said.

"I was hoping you would mull it over while I'm away. It would be the perfect timing. I've warned my agent that I may take some time off after this job."

"Love, you're about to star in a Jean Mercier film. It hardly makes sense now of all times. Isn't this the kind of film you've always hoped to do?"

"Well yes, but . . ."

"This role will open a lot of doors. Having a child now will only derail your brilliant career."

"I can still work. Lots of women do it. I've been acting nonstop for more than twenty years. A break wouldn't be the worst thing. It's exhausting, you know, spending your life portraying other people. Like I said last night, we could try when I return. Should things go well . . ."

"Charlotte, you're forty years old. Doubtful it would be as easy as you think. Aren't we a little past our prime to be starting with all of this?"

"Many women get pregnant in their early forties. Adoption is also a possibility if we have trouble. I downloaded some information," she said, grabbing a pile of papers off the coffee table.

He kissed her forehead and said, "I've got to go, love. Leave the papers and I'll look them over, but honestly, I suspect you'll feel differently when you return. You're an artist, Charlotte. You always return to the thing you're most devoted to: acting. A few days of filming and you'll forget all about this."

"Maybe, but . . ."

"Text me when you get there so I know you've arrived safely. Have a wonderful shoot. Get immersed, lose yourself," he said as he dashed out the door, leaving her clutching the unread papers. She took a steadying breath and looked around the large, open-concept flat they had shared for years, the walls covered with art gathered during her travels, reminders of the life she had chosen.

"YOU'VE GOT A PHENOMENAL ASS. Turn around, baby. I want to do you from behind," Michael instructed, grabbing her hips and swiveling her around. "That's it, baby, that's it," he said, moving faster and faster until he groaned in ecstasy. He pulled back, patted her bottom, and said, "That was great."

"I still can't believe I'm here, in Michael Hennesey's apartment," she said, giggly and wide-eyed. "Your place is so modern, sleek, masculine. I guess that comes from being a bachelor. Maybe you need a woman's touch around here."

"I think we just covered that, babe," he replied with a chuckle.

"I've always had such a crush on you. I've watched you on television for years. When we met last night . . ."

"I'm gonna grab a water. You want something?"

"I'm fine," she replied, pulling the silk sheets up.

He put his underwear on, looked at her sensuously, and said, "You stay put."

6

He trotted to the kitchen and opened the refrigerator, catching sight of his reflection in the stainless steel and smoothing his hair. As he guzzled a bottled water, he noticed the message light flashing on his phone and decided to listen to his voicemail. The first message was from his driver, confirming his pickup time. The next message was from Lauren.

"Hi Michael, it's Lauren. Listen, Sophie wants to go to an arts camp in August. I'd appreciate it if you could send some money. I've emailed you the invoice. No need to call back. Please have your assistant wire it over. Thanks."

He looked despondently at the callback number. His finger hovered over the dial button, but instead he sighed heavily and set the phone down on the counter. He strutted back to the bedroom, trying to remember the name of the woman waiting in his bed.

"Hey, baby," he said, slipping under the covers beside her.

"Didn't you say you're leaving town today to film a movie?" she asked.

"Later, but we have time for round two," he said, pulling her body against his.

"HE DID A GREAT JOB WITH YOUR HAIR. You look just like a young, brown-eyed Marilyn Monroe," the makeup artist said as she adhered the final false eyelash.

"I don't know how I'm going to survive the next three months without my glam squad," Willow said, admiring her newly styled platinum blonde hair.

"I'm sure you'll be in good hands with the makeup artists and hairstylists on set."

"It's not the same. We've all been friends for so long," she replied, sipping her light Caramel Frappuccino, careful not to mess up her lipstick. "You guys always take care of me. But Jean's people were awfully specific with my management team—no entourages allowed."

"Beauty, you're starring in a Jean Mercier film. Don't you worry about a thing."

"All I do is worry," Willow replied, looking down at her nervously wringing hands. "I don't know why he cast me. I've never done anything like this before. I mean, I'll be acting with Albie Hughes, Finn Forrester, and Charlotte Reed! They're *real actors*." She gazed straight ahead at her reflection. "I look at this girl in the mirror and wonder who the hell she thinks she's fooling. This is so far out of my league. What if . . ."

"What if you have some confidence for a change and realize that you're a brilliant performer? I know it's not my place to say, but Brian's always trying to get you to take jobs where you strut around like some kind of sex symbol. There's so much more to you. You're multitalented. Maybe this film will finally prove it to you."

"I'm afraid that . . ."

"If you're worried that you'll start drinking . . ."

"No, it's not that. I don't expect anyone to believe me, but I really have a handle on that and I know what to do if I get in trouble. I just don't want to embarrass myself. I've had enough public humiliation for a lifetime."

Just then, Willow's manager, Brian, came bounding into the room with his assistant. He pecked her on the forehead and said, "Doll, you look gorgeous. The car is waiting outside. Before you leave, we need to discuss some opportunities that have come in. Now that you're ready to perform again, everyone wants you."

"Yeah, okay," she said.

"*Maxim* wants you for another cover shoot. They're thinking topless with long hair extensions that will cover your breasts."

"Oh, I don't know . . ."

"It's major exposure. If you want more Hollywood roles, you know the score," Brian said.

"What else?" she asked.

"There's a guest spot in a music video. You'll be reprising your role for the fifth installment of that horror franchise; this time you can really cash in. Then there's one more that you may not like, but hear me out."

"What is it?"

"A cruise ship line is putting together a slate of former pop stars for a spring cruise through the Caribbean. You'd just have to perform a few of your old songs, complete with backup dancers. When you hear what they're willing to pay you . . ."

"Brian, none of this is what I want. When I came back to work, I told you that I wanted it to be different this time. Then I landed this Jean Mercier film . . ."

"Well, that's just it, doll. This film came out of nowhere. We still don't know how you got it. We need to cash in on this momentum and build your brand again. Don't I always take care of you?"

"Yes, but . . . I need some time to think things over."

"They really need answers to these invitations. I'll go ahead with the bookings, and you can always back out."

"That makes me look flaky. I don't want to earn a bad reputation again. Please just wait until . . ."

"Listen, the car is outside. I'll ride with you, and we can chat more on the way to the airport."

"Fine," she said reluctantly, staring at her reflection and trying desperately to recognize the face staring back at her.

FINN DROPPED HIS LUGGAGE IN THE foyer as the doorbell rang. He opened the door, visibly surprised to see Savannah standing there, decked out in a tube top, skinny jeans, and stiletto heels. "Uh, hey," he mumbled.

"Hey. Can I come in?" she asked.

"Of course," he replied.

"Looks like you're all packed and ready to go," she observed, gesturing at the luggage.

"Yeah. The driver will be here soon."

"Well, you're taking your own private jet. I'm sure it'll wait if you're a few minutes late. We need to talk."

He sighed and said, "Yeah, fine. Let's go sit in the living room. Can I get you something to drink?"

"I'm fine, thanks," she replied. They plopped onto the couch. "Listen, Finn, I've been thinking about what you said last night, and I know you didn't mean it."

"Savannah . . ."

"It's been good between us."

"I've been away doing films for most of our relationship. If I hadn't been on the road nonstop, we never would have . . ."

"I've kept your bed warm, haven't I?" she asked, touching his hand.

"Savannah . . ."

"Finn, we've been together for nearly two years. You can't just throw that away."

"I'm not. I've tried to make things work. The truth is that we should have split up a long time ago. It's not right between us, and I don't think it ever was. We've just been biding our time, spinning our wheels. Our relationship isn't going anywhere."

"Babe, I've told you before, I want to move in with you. Think about it! No more house sitters when you're on the road—I'll be here. We can get married in a big blowout bash. I saw the most incredible ring in the window at Cartier. I can text you a picture of it, and . . ."

"Savannah . . ."

"We're perfect for each other," she continued, playfully running her hand up his arm and through his light brown hair. "You need someone who doesn't care that you're always off doing movies, someone who looks the part and can accompany you down the red carpet and do the whole Hollywood glamour thing."

"I don't care about that stuff. Never have."

"Don't be silly. Of course you do," she said, fluffing her blonde hair. "I know what this is really about. When I got home last night, I was thinking to myself, *Why is Finn doing this now when everything is so perfect?*"

"It's not perfect, not to me," he said softly.

Ignoring his comment, she continued, "You're going to be away on location for three long months. You're worried that if you're attached, you won't be able to have sex."

"That's what you think?" he asked.

"Babe, I know what your sexual appetite is like," she said, tousling his hair. "You're a big star, you don't see why you should go without. I get it. So, I've decided you can get blow jobs."

"What?" he bellowed, his eyes wide.

"I know that local girls and extras always hit on you. My God, you're Finn Forrester, after all! Everyone wants you, and well they should. Why should you have to go without basic satisfaction? I'm cool with it."

"You're cool with me being intimate with other women? Do you even hear yourself? This is exactly the problem. Think about . . ."

"Babe, I'm just being realistic and trying to give you what you want. You're a big movie star, of course you need to be allowed to bend the rules. I'd have a problem with it if you fuck other women, but if you want to get your dick sucked a few times, it's fine. I totally get it. Now that this problem is solved, there's no reason to break up. Go make your film and get your rocks off if you need to. Think of me. When you get back, we can focus on us and our future."

He shook his head in disbelief. "Savannah, this isn't what I want."

"There's no reason to do anything rash. We've had two years together. We've been happy. Just wait until you come back before you make any decisions. I'm sure you'll feel differently once you see how much you miss me and you realize how cool this arrangement is. Not every woman would be this understanding. Everything I do is all for you."

"I don't even know how to respond to this."

"Don't say anything. It's all good. I'll be here when you get back."

"Look, there's no point in hammering this conversation to death now, but we need to have a serious talk when I get home," Finn said. "The time apart will do us both good. In my heart, I know there's something better out there for each of us."

ELLA TRAIPSED INTO HER LOFT CARRYING a bouquet of purple and white flowers, the afternoon sun shining brightly in the small space, a soft breeze blowing through the open balcony doors. She played her voicemail while arranging the flowers in a vase.

"*Ma chérie*, it's Jean. I've been in Sweden for a few days, getting everything set up. We've cleared out an old inn a few miles from the filming location; I'll be staying there with the lead actors. It's an enormous old house, buttercup yellow. You would love it. The dining room has a dance floor, an old piano in the corner, and a fully stocked bar. Lots of spectacular nature around for you to explore. Please come. I'll save you the best room."

"It does sound nice," she mumbled to herself. "Hmm . . ."

12

She sent him a text message:

I'm tempted. Have a few things to do in Paris. Maybe I'll come out in a week or two. Hope my room has a writing desk. Good luck with the shoot. Love, Ella.

 **CHAPTER 2**

"**Y**ou're all set," Maja said.

"Not bad," Michael replied. "Thanks. You really know what you're doing. How long have you been a makeup artist?"

"A few years. This was easy. You have perfect bone structure," she said, smiling coyly.

"I hope we can get to know each other better," he replied, looking at her suggestively.

She giggled. "The hairstylist will be here any minute. Can I get you anything while you wait?"

"I'm good, thanks," he said, picking up his bottled water and taking a sip through a straw.

As soon as she left the makeup trailer, Michael turned to Finn in the seat beside him and said, "God, these Swedish chicks are hot. Friendly too. I dig Maja."

Finn looked up from the script he was studying and laughed. "Honestly, I hadn't noticed. I'm trying to prepare."

"You've done so many films. This will be a piece of cake. There's barely any dialogue to learn, seems like we'll be filling in the blanks as we go."

"It's the leanest script I've ever received. Hard to understand what the film is even about, other than a family disintegrating at a party. Some kind of metaphor, I guess."

Finn ran his hand through his hair. "Acting alongside someone like Albie Hughes . . . well, it's something I've always hoped for. Working with Jean too, of course. I've heard he really pushes his actors. That's what I've been looking for, a chance to do something different and grow."

"Yeah, my agent thought it would be a good change for me. Playing a TV heartthrob certainly has its advantages; it catapults you into instant fame, and there's never a shortage of beautiful women. I just don't want to get stuck." He leaned closer and said, "But don't get so lost in your work that you miss all the eye candy. This Scandinavian, blue-eyed, blonde thing isn't to be missed."

Finn chuckled. "Actually, I sort of have a girlfriend back in LA, Savannah. Not that she'd care if I were with someone else."

"Sounds like a win-win."

"I wouldn't say that. We've been together for nearly two years. She's been pressuring me to get engaged."

"Yikes!"

Finn laughed again. "The truth is, I've wanted to settle down for a long time, but I don't think she's the one. I tried to break up with her before I left for this shoot, but . . ."

"Then take it from me, don't let these little Swedish beauties pass you by. See what else is out there, have some fun. Enjoy the benefits of being a movie star."

Before Finn could respond, the hairstylist came in. "Sorry to keep you both waiting. I'll be quick. They're ready for you on set."

"WOAH," MICHAEL SAID AS HE AND Finn walked into the massive 20,000-square-foot estate that had been rented for the shoot. The equipment, crew, and extras couldn't detract from the grandeur of the high ceilings, crystal chandeliers, pristinely preserved parquet floors, and enormous windows overlooking the expansive grassy property. Beyond the rolling lawn was the crystal-clear sea, dotted with birds. All the action was in the grand ballroom, where they'd be filming the lengthy party scene over the next several weeks.

"I'd like to say a few words before we begin," Jean said in his thick French accent. The entire cast and crew quieted down in reverence. "For those of you who haven't met him, this is my assistant, Drew. I'm sure he can help with any issues you encounter." Drew smiled and nodded at everyone, and Jean continued, "The party scene is the heart of the film. Let's get it right, *oui*? We want to take people on a journey that begins lavish and lush but turns inward, twisting on itself, becoming increasingly dark. I'd like to call each of the stars to the center of the room. Albie Hughes, playing the family's benevolent patriarch. Finn Forrester, in the role of the disgruntled eldest son, and Charlotte Reed as his depressed wife. Willow Barnes as the illegitimate daughter, and Michael Hennesey as her drunken, gold-digging husband."

Everyone clapped.

"Okay," Jean continued. "I'm not one for sentimentality. We're starting with the cocktail hour. Let's get to work."

The actors, all dressed in formal wear, quickly dispersed. They spent a few minutes mingling before Jean yelled, "Places, everyone. Rolling . . . Action!"

Finn looked at Charlotte, utterly confused. They hadn't done any blocking or rehearsals. He whispered to her, "You look over there, and . . ."

"Cut!" Jean hollered. "Finn, no talking."

"I'm sorry. I . . ."

"No talking!" Jean repeated sternly.

Albie leaned over and whispered to the others, "This is how he works. You just have to go with it. If it helps, I never have a clue what's going on either."

Finn laughed.

"Starting again. Places, everyone," Jean called. "Rolling . . . Action!"

They ran through the scene with great confusion until Jean yelled, "Cut!"

The actors milled about aimlessly, looking at one another for some sort of sign as to how things were going.

"Less acting, everyone. You are meant to be at a party, not on a bloody stage reciting a soliloquy. Don't force it. Be natural, jovial. Starting again. Places!" Jean yelled.

Things continued in much the same manner until Jean wrapped filming for the day, instructing the lead actors to meet in the dining room back at the inn for dinner in one hour. They all shuffled out together, chatting about the shoot on the way to their trailers.

"I fear I was terrible," Charlotte said.

"You weren't, although I apologize if I was. This will take some getting used to," Finn said.

"That was the worst day I can recall ever having on a set. I've never felt so lost. I had so wanted to impress Jean, and now . . ."

Albie chuckled and said, "You'll all get used to how Jean does things, I promise. There were a couple of beautiful moments, but you were probably too stuck in your own heads to notice. That's all he's after, the moments. He's teasing them out of us. Don't worry, it'll all work out in the end. He knows what he's doing."

"He seemed pissed off all day," Michael remarked.

"Don't expect that to change," Albie replied with a laugh.

"I think it was my fault. I couldn't calm my nerves," Willow said softly. "I bet he regrets casting me. I haven't worked in years. I'm sorry if . . ."

"Now, now, none of this rubbish. Toughen up, for Christ's sake. You're professionals. What you all need to understand is that Jean is intense when he's working. He's not one for coddling," Albie explained. "He won't hold your hand or pass out gold stars, but the films I've done with him have been the finest of my career. This was only the first day."

"You really respect him," Finn said.

"Wouldn't be here if I didn't. Being part of a Jean Mercier film is an honor. You just have to figure out how to put up with his eccentricities."

They all laughed.

Albie continued, "You'll get to know him better over dinner each night. He's not so intimidating once he has a couple of whiskeys in him."

THE ACTORS MEANDERED INTO THE dining room to find Jean sitting at a round table in the center of the room, with a semicircular booth and several chairs pulled up. Jean was sprawled out in the booth. The waiter came over and handed him a drink. "Here's your bourbon neat, sir."

"What's everyone else having?" Jean asked as they all sat down.

"A white wine, please," Charlotte said.

"Sparkling water," Willow said.

"I'll have what he's having," Albie said, gesturing at Jean's glass.

"Same for me, please," Finn replied.

"Vodka tonic," Michael said.

"Very good," the waiter said, placing a basket of bread and a bowl of olives on the table before scurrying away.

"Quite something to have this large room to ourselves, isn't it?" Jean said. "I always rent out an inn or a house to share with the cast. Living together is part of the adventure of filmmaking. This place is a bit worse for wear, but of course, so am I."

"This place is very quaint, homey," Charlotte said. "The antique furniture in my room is lovely."

"The grounds are beautiful. It's so peaceful here," Finn added.

They all smiled faintly, quietly fidgeting in their seats.

Jean chuckled. "You all need to loosen up and relax."

"It's just . . . well, we're wondering if today went as you hoped," Finn said.

"Don't worry about it," Jean replied with a dismissive wave of his hand.

The actors all exchanged nervous glances as the waiter served their drinks.

"I propose a toast," Jean said, raising his glass. "To our film."

"Cheers!" they all said, clinking glasses.

Albie took a swig of his bourbon and said, "Jean, everyone's feeling a bit shell-shocked after today. They're not yet used to the way you work. Why don't you tell them about your first film?"

Jean chuckled. "I made a short film as my final project in film school. A piece of shit, really, shot completely with a handheld camera, but it was quite different than what other people were doing, perhaps even a bit vulgar. Sure enough, it took home a few prizes at the festivals that year, causing quite a stir."

Everyone sat listening eagerly.

"After that, there were all kinds of opportunities for financial backing. I knew the only way to control my art was to be a producer, so I took out a loan and started my own small production company, the same company that has made all my films to date. We had a shoestring budget for our first feature-length picture, *Pump*, an extended version of my short film. It was an exploration of love and sex, emphasis on the sex."

"The press labeled it pornography," Albie said with a chuckle.

"They weren't wrong," Jean replied, bursting into laughter.

"I've seen it. Very gritty," Michael said.

"I've seen it too. Daring," Finn added.

"Yes," Charlotte agreed. "I've studied all your work."

"It was rough as hell, but it certainly made a point," Jean said. "The press was so repulsed by it that they gave it a much bigger spotlight than it would have otherwise enjoyed. People can be so absurdly provincial about sexual matters, especially the Americans. It received a slew of award nominations simply because of the commotion the press inadvertently caused. That pissed them off something awful."

Albie cracked up, the others following suit.

"Tell them about the first day of filming," Albie said. "Might shed some perspective on today."

"The first scene we shot was an explicit sex act between the two lead characters. You should have seen the actors' faces when they learned what we'd be starting with, only moments after they'd met. They were nude, covered only with groin cloths when I yelled action, no blocking or any of that other garbage. They hardly knew what to do, as if they were suddenly virgins. I must say, I had a good laugh over it, although I do know it was a bit wicked of me." He took a sip of his drink. "So you see, today wasn't so bad. I've gone easy on you. All you had to do was make small talk at a party."

They all laughed, their shoulders relaxing a bit.

The waiter came by and announced, "The buffet is open."

"Excellent. Let's get some food, order another round, and then we can talk about something other than the damn film. You all look like a fun and obscenely pampered group; I want to hear your stories of excess and self-indulgence. I've got some doozies of my own you may be able to coax out of me."

CHAPTER 3

Nearly two weeks into the shoot, they had settled into a nightly routine: when the dishes were cleared, they were served another round of drinks and settled in for conversation and laughter. As usual, it was bourbon for Jean, Finn, and Albie, vodka tonic for Michael, white wine for Charlotte, and sparkling water for Willow. Just as the drinks arrived, Jean's assistant, Drew, popped in to drop off some papers.

"Stay, have a drink," Jean commanded.

"I'll just have water," Drew said, taking a seat as Jean slid him a glass.

"Cheers," they all said, raising their glasses.

After taking a sip, Finn looked across the table at Jean and said, "So, it's been almost two weeks. You ever gonna tell us what this movie is about or if you're even getting what you want?"

"Don't worry about it," Jean replied.

Used to that response, they all laughed.

Just then, Finn noticed a strikingly beautiful woman who looked to be in her early thirties sweep into the room. She was breathtaking in a sleeveless black silk jumpsuit, cinched at the waist, with several long, sparkling chains hanging from her neck, light brown hair in natural spiral curls flowing down her back, and large, piercing green eyes. He couldn't take his eyes off her. Michael caught him staring and looked over, also transfixed by the beautiful stranger. Drew winked at her, signaling to the others that he knew her. She put her finger to her mouth as if to keep her presence a secret as she tiptoed toward the table. She rested her alabaster hands on Jean's biceps, leaned over his shoulder, and purred in his ear, "Darling, I'm here."

He jumped up from the table, grinning from ear to ear, picked her up, and whirled her around in the air. She flung her head back, giggling with abandon. When he eventually put her down, he said, "Thank you for coming, *ma chérie*."

"Well, your request was hardly subtle. You left a dozen messages and followed up with a private jet. I assumed you must need me desperately. Or were you just being overly dramatic, as you're prone to do?"

"Let's sit down. You can have a drink and meet the actors. If you're hungry, I'll have the kitchen prepare something, whatever you desire."

"First things first. We dance," she said, looking at him coyly.

Jean turned to Drew and said, "Put one of our songs on, *s'il vous plaît*."

Drew pulled out his phone and paired it to the speaker he'd brought along. Soon, Elton John's "Goodbye Yellow Brick Road" filled the room. With the opening chords, Jean took the mysterious woman's hand and escorted her to the dance floor. They waltzed dramatically across the room, their smiles growing with each whirl. Each time the refrain began, the woman put her back against Jean's chest and they swayed back and forth, their arms extended wide, and then he grabbed her hand and twirled her around during the chorus. Finn and the rest of group sat mesmerized as the unpredictable director completely transformed before their eyes, gracefully moving around the room with the enchanting stranger. As the final refrain ended, he picked her up and spun her once more, both smiling widely. He carefully put her down, and they whispered conspiratorially to each other.

"My God, who is she?" Finn asked quietly.

"Gabriella Sinclair, but everyone calls her Ella. Thirty-four years old. An American philosopher," Drew said.

"She's a brilliant philosopher. An artist, really. She presents her theories through literary writing like Simone de Beauvoir or Jean-Paul Sartre, although she's much more, um, risqué," Charlotte added. "We've never met, but I've been reading her work for years. She's fearless, daring, marches to the beat of her own drum."

"He looks like he's completely in love with her," Michael remarked. "Are they . . ."

Drew shook his head. "They're close friends. She's his muse, or perhaps he's hers."

"I've enjoyed the pleasure of her company before. A Jean Mercier production finds flight when she enters the picture. Ella's presence on set changes everything," Albie said. "She's a real artist through and through, the embodiment of inspiration. And not bad to look at either," he added, taking a swig of his drink.

The men laughed. Willow smiled while Charlotte rolled her eyes discreetly.

"Oh, come on, now. I'm an old man. I must have some pleasure from time to time, even if it is just looking," Albie teased, touching Charlotte's arm. "Besides, Ella doesn't mind. She has an extraordinarily strong sexual energy and a real bohemian spirit."

"Her writing is quite provocative," Charlotte said, the trace of a smile appearing on her demure face.

Finished with their whisperings, Jean and Ella walked over to the table, his arm comfortably slung around her waist. "Everyone, it is my great honor to introduce the one and only Gabriella Sinclair."

"Please, call me Ella," she said in a silvery voice. She darted over to Albie and hugged him affectionately. "I hope we have some fun this time around," Finn heard her whisper, "like at the Barcelona shoot or that time in the Cotswolds." He patted her hand and chuckled. She kissed the top of his head and returned to Jean's side.

"Ella, obviously you know Albie and Drew, and I'm sure you recognize the rest of these scene stealers," Jean said.

"Very nice to meet you," Michael said, the others nodding in agreement.

"Likewise," she replied, her smile revealing a dimple in the right cheek of her heart-shaped face. "So, let me guess: you're at the part of the shoot when you're wondering what the hell you're doing here."

They all laughed.

"Pretty much sums it up," Finn said, raising his sea-colored eyes to meet her gaze. Her eyes lingered on his face for a moment before turning to Jean.

"The driver is in the entryway with my luggage. Where shall I direct him?" she asked.

"I saved you the best room with a large writing desk, as you requested," he replied, gesturing at Drew to give her the key. "Number seven, on the second floor."

"Please order me whatever you're drinking. I'll be back in just a moment." She turned to the group and said, "I'm really looking forward to getting to know you all."

They all smiled and nodded politely.

Jean plopped back down with an entirely different energy

than they had seen before. He called to the waiter to bring another bourbon neat. Everyone stared at him, their mouths slightly agape.

He sipped his drink and explained, "Ella has this effect on people."

"It's more the effect she has on you," Michael said. "Your entire demeanor changed when she arrived."

"There is no one on this earth who brings me greater joy. All who know her feel the same. She's got a fire about her. To be fully alive, that is truly something," he said dreamily. He paused and continued, "She understands what it means to make art that asks the big questions. Few possess what she does. She's one of a kind and brings a certain *je ne sais quoi* to a project."

Finn saw Michael glancing around the table, no doubt noticing that everyone looked as intrigued as he was. "You looked completely smitten with her. Is she your . . . ?"

"My lover? No," he said, shaking his head. "She has rules about sex. Won't sleep with me."

Michael and Finn each raised an eyebrow, eager to hear more.

Ella came flitting back into the room. She slid into the booth next to Jean just as the waiter served her drink.

"Ella," Jean said, "tell them about your fucking rules."

The actors' jaws hit the floor, shocked by his brazen question.

"Gee, you can't even let a girl have a drink and get settled in," she joked.

Albie chuckled.

She turned to the group and said, "It's simple. You should only sleep with people you'll always love or people you'll never love."

Finn looked down, blushing. The others burst into laughter.

"I suppose that has a sort of logic to it," Willow mumbled.

Jean draped his arm around Ella and said, "Darling, if that were true, we'd be in bed right now."

"Oh, please! The only person you'll always love is *you*," she said matter-of-factly.

No one could stifle their laughter. Ella shrugged, picked up her glass, and took a sip. "Ooh, that's smooth," she remarked. Finn noticed that Michael was practically undressing her with his eyes. He was staring too, although he tried to be far more subtle about it. He caught her eye, and they gazed at one another for a moment.

"So, have you come here to save us?" Jean asked.

"You don't need saving, my darling," she said, playfully tousling his hair. "This is merely a chance to inspire each other. I'm writing a series of four short books and figured being away in the country would be a good change of scenery. I'll stay for the next two and a half months until you wrap the shoot; I'll do what I can, but I'll be busy with my own work." She paused, dramatically widened her eyes, and looked straight at Jean. "Listen, I expect your feedback on my draft manuscripts. This isn't all about you."

He laughed. "Looking forward to it. I imagine I'm in for a treat."

"Good. Then I'm in."

"Will you come to set tomorrow morning? There will be a shuttle van taking people between the set and the inn all day. We start filming at ten."

"Darling, you know I don't punch a time card, but I'll pop by."

He kissed her cheek. "And group dinners each night."

"Yes, of course. I know how you operate," she replied. "It would help if you told me what the film is about before I stop by the set." She turned to the group. "Well, I can't ask you guys. You probably haven't a clue other than some half-baked script you got!"

Drew laughed, and the actors followed suit.

She turned to Jean. "So, do tell. What is your latest masterpiece about?"

He shook his head. "I want your pure impression." He turned to the others and instructed, "You're all under strict orders. Do not show her your scripts."

Ella rolled her eyes. "Fine, we can play it that way. Will you at least tell me the title?"

"No," Jean said, gently tugging on one of the curls hanging on the side of her face, mesmerized like a child as it bounced back up.

She giggled and pointed to a pack of cigarettes on the table. "May I?"

"Please, be my guest," Finn said, holding out the pack and flipping it open for her.

She slid a cigarette out, tilted her chin downward, and softly said, "Thank you," as their eyes met.

"My pleasure," he replied, staring at her as if they were the only two souls in the room. He retrieved a silver lighter and leaned across the table to light it for her.

She exhaled a line of smoke and said, "*Merci.*" He smiled in return and took his seat again. "So," she said, "we can't talk about the film. What shall we discuss? Who hates each other? Who's sleeping together?"

 **CHAPTER 4**

The next morning, Finn meandered into the dining room shortly after eight o'clock. As usual, Albie was sitting in the corner by the window, reading the newspaper as he munched on buttered toast with orange marmalade. They nodded politely at one another. Across the room, Ella stretched her arms as she gazed out the window, notebooks strewn across a nearby table. She was wearing a white cropped T-shirt that showed off her slim waist, wide-legged jeans that flared at the bottom, elongating her frame, and beaded sandals, revealing several toe rings. Her thick hair was pulled into a loose bun at the nape of her neck. She looked effortlessly beautiful, and he caught himself staring as she turned toward him. They made eye contact, and she smiled and waved him over.

"Good morning," he said.

"Good morning. Please join me."

"Are you sure? I don't want to disturb you," he said, gesturing to the notebooks on the table.

She scooped up the journals and pushed them aside in a pile. "Nonsense. I'd love the company."

He sat down and looked around the quiet room. "I've been on my own most mornings. Albie likes to be left alone, which I understand. Willow and Charlotte have breakfast sent up to their rooms. Michael often finds his way here in a panicked rush because he's always pushing the clock to make his call time, and Jean is on set before any of us are even awake."

She laughed. "When he's obsessed, he's obsessed."

A waiter came over with a fresh pot of coffee and filled Finn's mug. "What can I get you both this morning?"

"After you," Finn said.

"A soft-boiled egg and some fruit, and more hot water for my tea, please," Ella said.

"Oatmeal with berries, please," Finn said. When the waiter walked away, Finn continued, "This place doesn't exactly have a state-of-the-art gym, so I run in the mornings and then find myself famished by breakfast."

"I'm sure this isn't the kind of living situation you're used to when you're on location. It's seriously lacking in glamour, although I find it quite charming. There's something peaceful and cozy about this place. It feels a bit like a hug."

He smiled and shook his head. "I've done about a hundred feature films, but this one is a first in many ways. Even though this place lacks some modern touches, the charm isn't lost on me. It's like we're all living in someone's house together, not in some austere hotel. I'm really enjoying spending time with Jean and the cast. It's starting to feel kind of like a family, just like in the film, which I guess is his logic."

She smiled. "Well, you won't need to eat alone anymore unless you choose to. I never miss breakfast, though I'm usually so swept up in my work that I forget to have lunch."

"What are you working on? You mentioned a four-book project."

"I'm interested in what brings human beings pleasure and what that experience is like. I have a theory that there are only four things human beings experience in their wholeness: sex, art, food, and nature. Culture can get in the way and influence, obscure, and subvert our experience of these things, and in fact, it usually does. Yet there is at least the possibility, the potentiality that we may experience them with a oneness that doesn't exist elsewhere."

Finn was completely enthralled, his eyes glued to her as she spoke.

She continued, "It's why these things have the power to bring us tremendous pleasure like nothing else—they make us feel the splendor of being alive. When they are good and when we're truly free and open to the experience, these things feed our souls, awaken our senses, and propel us to states of calm and ecstasy."

"I've never thought about that before, but now I find myself reflecting on my own life and the things that have brought me bliss. I'm completely bowled over. This is fascinating."

She smiled and said, "Thank you. So, I'm writing four short books, one on each of those topics. Together, it's a study in human pleasure and this idea I have about oneness."

"What about love?" he asked. "Do you think love brings us pleasure?"

"There's nothing more devastatingly beautiful or pleasurable than love, I imagine, although I'm hardly an expert." He smiled warmly at her and she continued, "It's incredibly difficult to pin down. Love means so many different things and is experienced in innumerable ways. How do we define it without limiting it? There's a materiality or physicality to the topics I've selected that's impossible to have with an abstract concept like love."

"I see," he said.

"Still, it naturally creeps in when writing about these four topics. Love is part of all of them, with sex perhaps being the most obvious. Sex between people truly in love with one another can bring enormous pleasure, both physically and spiritually. Or so I'm told."

"I think so too. Or at least I hope so." They held each other's gaze for a long, comfortable moment. Eventually, he said, "I apologize if this is a stupid question, but will you use the same writing style for all four books? Are they meant to mirror each other?"

She smiled brightly. "That's a fantastic question. I've never been what you'd call a traditional writer. My writing merges different styles and structures—essays, fiction, plays. Creative thinking demands creative writing. I imagine the books will each be close to the same length but with differing approaches. Whatever works to deliver the ideas, you know? So far, I have rough drafts of the volumes on sex and art. I'm hoping to refine those while I'm here, with Jean's input, and this feels like the ideal place to start on the nature book."

Finn turned his attention out the window. "The grounds here are spectacular. The sun doesn't set until around ten o'clock, and even after, it never really gets totally dark this time of year. I find the light in the evening to be particularly beautiful. Maybe one night after dinner we could take a stroll."

"I'd love that," she said.

Just then, the waiter delivered their breakfast.

"Bon appétit," she said.

"Bon appétit," he replied.

Before they could take a bite of their food, Michael came barreling into the room. His eyes went straight to Ella like a laser, as if he had been looking for her.

"Ah, it looks like you wouldn't have been alone this morning after all," she said to Finn.

"I have a feeling I'm not the one he was hoping to see," he whispered.

She giggled.

"Michael, come join us," Finn called.

"Thanks," Michael said, dropping in the chair beside him. He threw his hand up to signal to the waiter and then hollered out his order: "An espresso and an egg white omelet with spinach, no dairy." He turned to Ella and said, "You look lovely today. How was your first night in our humble abode?"

"Fine, thank you. I was glad for a good night's sleep. It's so quiet here. There's nothing like the country, especially when you're a city girl."

"Where do you live?" Michael asked.

"All over. I rarely stay in one place for long. I've been renting a little flat in Paris, but then Jean started pestering me."

"We're all looking forward to having you on set today," Michael said. "If you have any questions about the film, feel free to stop by my trailer and we can speak privately."

She glanced at Finn, and he watched her eyes linger on his smile. Moving past Michael's invitation, she picked up her small spoon and tapped on the egg's light brown shell. "What is it about that sound that's so satisfying?" she asked.

Finn smiled.

She stuck her spoon into the egg with consideration, slowly penetrating the white until she reached the runny yolk. She lifted the spoon, dripping in glistening, orange yolk, looked Finn directly in his inviting eyes, and said, "See? There's something so pleasurable about that, and I haven't even taken a bite."

She and Finn smiled at each other like two people in on a private joke.

"What did I miss?" Michael asked, a bewildered expression on his face.

THEY WERE IN THE MIDDLE OF SHOOTING the same party scene they'd been working on since the first day of filming when Ella strolled onto set that afternoon. When Jean yelled, "Cut!" the band stopped playing and the actors wandered away from their marks.

Jean flashed a genuine, broad smile at the sight of her, something the actors had never seen on set before. As Ella flitted over, Michael whispered to Finn, "God, she's gorgeous."

"That she is. I've never seen anyone as beautiful. I was speaking with her this morning about her work. Fascinating stuff. She's a brilliant woman," Finn replied, staring shamelessly.

Still gawking, Michael said, "She has something special, some quality about her. I can't put my finger on it, but it's intoxicating."

"Be careful," Finn cautioned. "The last thing you want to do is piss off the filmmaker."

Michael shrugged. "They're just friends. He said so himself."

"She's important to him. He went to a lot of trouble to have her here. I don't think he'd want her, well, upset in any way."

"I can be very charming, I'll have you know. Women go crazy for me," Michael replied in a joking tone.

Finn didn't respond. It was clear to him that Ella had no interest in Michael.

After Ella and Jean chatted for a minute, Jean yelled, "Places, everyone! We're going to run it again."

Finn glanced at Ella, and she smiled at him before looking away with a bashfulness that surprised him.

"Rolling . . . Action!" Jean called.

They began shooting the dancing scene again as multiple cameras spun around the room, capturing it from different angles. Ella stood on the sidelines to watch the action, but after only three minutes, she pecked Jean on each cheek and quietly slipped out.

When they cut the scene, Michael said to Finn, "She didn't stay very long."

"We couldn't have been that bad," Finn joked. "We didn't even have any dialogue."

Michael laughed. "What exactly do you think she's meant to do here? Jean desperately wanted her to join us, but then she drifts in and out for a few minutes in the middle of the day. I don't get it."

Finn shrugged. "Beats me. But I have a feeling that whatever she brings to a project is something we'll all be grateful for."

AFTER A LONG DAY, THEY ALL SAT DOWN to break bread, as had become their tradition. The women and Jean sat in the booth, and the others sat in surrounding chairs. The staff promptly served drinks and announced, "The dinner buffet is open."

"Shall we toast?" Ella asked, raising her glass.

"Before we indulge ourselves, let's hear your thoughts," Jean said. "Have you figured out what the film is about?"

Ella smiled coyly, all eyes upon her. "All right," she said, rolling the glass of amber liquid between her palms. She leaned back and continued, "Obviously you were film-ing a party scene, but not just any party. It's a massively grand celebration befitting the obscenely rich, and since there were no bridal gowns or caskets, it must be a birthday. His, I imagine," she said, gesturing at Albie.

Everyone smiled, absolutely riveted.

Jean smirked. "Well, that was easy. Even *they* know that. Tell them something they don't know."

"Ah, good. Then I'm right so far," she replied. "Well, you always use metaphor and symbolism to examine one theme central to the human condition—love, sex, death, violence, the environment. This time you're trying to tackle the biggest theme of them all, which is why you wanted me here. Your film is about the meaning of life itself. Given your dire view of the species, it's about the tragedy of human life," she said, crinkling her nose and giggling.

Jean glanced down and shook his head in wonder. He looked up, his eyes on Ella, and caressed her cheek. "*Oui, ma chérie.* Tell them more."

She smiled. "It's about the meaning or meaninglessness of a single life, and by extension, the human race. It's about our struggle to matter, and the deep fear we hold that perhaps we do not, that we could not. I imagine there will be an exploration of regret, missed opportunities, pride, and longing." She paused and added, "The party scene is the center of the film. It's trivial, meant to imply that our lives are often trivial. The characters will start coming apart at the seams because, deep down, they know it too."

Jean smirked, faced the group, and said, "She is exactly right. It's an exploration of the meaning of human life, which of course is impossible to capture, and thus is a great white whale of a beast."

"Oh my God," Finn mumbled. "It all makes sense now. The script, the . . ."

"My character represents death, mortality," Albie said, as if he were figuring it out as each word left his mouth.

"My character must be meant to represent hope or naïveté," Willow said. "She still believes that a human being can matter, even in the face of all the pettiness and conflict she has with the others. She continues to feel this way even though her family can't rise above their own pathetic, selfish desires and cruelty toward one another."

Ella smiled as the actors began to understand their part in the mysterious, grand plan that suddenly seemed clear as day.

"Did anyone show her a script?" Jean asked accusatorially.

They all shook their heads.

Jean turned to Ella and said, "The title. Have you guessed it?"

"Hmm, that's always tricky. Let me give it a try. You always use one-word titles, so I'm assuming that's the case here and you're not trying to bamboozle me."

He chuckled. "Go on."

All eyes were glued to Ella.

"The film is about life itself, but you wouldn't choose the word *life*. Too obvious, too pedestrian. Given your misanthropic views, it could be called *Doom* or *Wasteland*. Perhaps you've chosen to be more subtle, in which case something like *Fragile* would be the clear choice. But subtlety has never been your style, has it?" She crinkled her nose and giggled. "Because you have such a bleak view of humanity, some people don't appreciate your wonderful, ironic sense of humor. The media often misses that altogether. It's a pity; it's such a fantastic part of your personality and your art. If you were going to create a film about the tragedy of the human condition, you would give it a falsely uplifting title. Hmm. What could it be, given that the film centers around a party?" Her face lit up with recognition, and she put her hand on his shoulder. "Darling, I seized upon the title as soon as we began this conversation. I said the scene you were shooting today was not just any party but 'a massively grand celebration.' The title of the film is *Celebration*."

All the actors' mouths were hanging open, their eyes nearly popping out of their heads.

"Ah, I see I'm right," Ella said proudly.

"Holy shit," Michael said. "That was amazing. You're practically clairvoyant. You got all that from three minutes on set while we were dancing?"

"You're extraordinarily perceptive," Charlotte remarked.

Jean smiled and said, "She never misses a thing." He raised his glass. "Ella, would you like to do the honors?"

She held up her glass. "To making beautiful art and exploring the big questions."

"Cheers!" Jean exclaimed.

"*Santé!*"

"*Skål!*"

"Bottoms up," Ella said, and they all clinked glasses.

PEOPLE CASUALLY WANDERED OVER to the buffet, and Ella and Finn found themselves to be the last two perusing the spread. "The food here is actually pretty good, and they've been very accommodating. They always have vegetarian options for Charlotte."

Ella smiled. "I love Swedish food, especially the gravlax," she said, picking up the tongs.

"Have you spent much time in Sweden?"

"A fair amount. Stockholm is a great city. It's entirely walkable with gorgeous water views, and I simply adore the modern art museum. You?"

"For all the traveling I do, this is only my second time in this country. The last time I was here, I was stuck in a hotel doing press junkets," he replied. He noticed she was eyeing the dill potatoes and said, "May I?" as he picked up the serving spoon.

"Please," she replied.

"You really blew everyone's minds," he said as he served her a scoop of creamy potatoes. "I can't believe how much you inferred from the little you saw."

She shrugged. "I know how Jean's mind works."

He shook his head and said, "I'll never know how you figured out the title."

She flirtatiously gestured for him to come closer. He leaned in close enough to smell her floral perfume and feel her warm breath on his ear, and she whispered, "One of the cameramen had the title taped to his equipment."

Finn burst into laughter. When he could manage to get the words out, he said, "You really had Jean going. Hell, you had all of us going!"

"People believe what they want to believe. Besides, I must have some fun if he insists on playing his little mind games." She giggled and said, "Jean was right, after all, I never miss a thing. He just misinterpreted what that meant." She winked at him, and they both returned to the table smiling.

They all spent the next three hours eating, drinking, smoking, and telling stories. All the while, Finn couldn't take his eyes off Ella.

 **CHAPTER 5**

Ella waltzed into the dining room the next morning, her laptop under her arm. Albie was tucked away in the corner, his nose in a newspaper. Finn was sitting at the table they had shared the morning before. He smiled brightly and said, "I saved you a seat."

"Good morning," she said as she sat opposite him and placed her laptop to the side.

"Good morning. I took a chance you'd join me and ordered you a pot of tea."

"That was sweet. Thank you," she replied, filling her teacup.

"Working on your books?" he asked, gesturing at her computer.

"Yes. I'm making a few final edits, and then I'll give Jean copies of the sex and art volumes tomorrow for his feedback. Next, I'll start taking notes for the nature volume. What about you? Are you looking forward to filming today?"

"More than ever. We've all felt so lost during the shoot, not understanding what the film is about or what Jean wants. Now we get it. Plus, the way he works is so unconventional. His filming changes without warning. Suddenly, you're in the middle of a close-up you had no idea was coming. Without any blocking or rehearsals, it's all about feeling things out with the other actors. I thought I was a seasoned pro, but this is a totally new experience."

"Those are usually the best kinds of experiences, don't you think? Besides, you have all the tools you need. Just trust it and be open to the moment. Jean gave me a copy of the script last night, and I curled up in bed and read it. It's good. Couldn't put it down. It's going to be a beautiful work of art."

"Charlotte's really been having a tough time. She's such a professional, but she's never worked in this kind of free-form way before. On set, Jean isn't the most . . ."

"Complimentary? Supportive?" Ella said.

"Yeah," Finn replied.

"That's just his way. He hates acting, so he doesn't quite know how to remark on it, other than to tell his actors to stop doing it."

Finn laughed.

"I know he's a huge fan of Charlotte's work," Ella said. "He sees something special in each of you. When he writes a new script, he's considering the cast as he goes. The roles were developed with each of you in mind because of what you've achieved, but also because of what he sees inside you that maybe hasn't had a chance to come out yet. His shoots are meant to be an expansive experience for the actors."

Finn smiled. "It's why I took the job. When my agent told me that Jean Mercier wanted me for a film, I signed on without even seeing a script. I've been stuck in the block-buster world for too long. These days, there are so few filmmakers who are truly trying to create cinematic art. It was a chance I couldn't pass up."

"I hope you feel you've made the right choice."

"I do. I already know this is something special. I do feel bad for Charlotte, though. She takes her work very seriously. As you know, we're married in the film, so we have most of our scenes together. I can tell that Jean's . . ."

"Lack of manners?"

He laughed. "His manner of working is difficult for her. She keeps asking me if she's doing a good job. She wants to impress him but feels adrift."

"I'll whisper a little something in his ear. Don't worry, I won't betray your confidence. I know he wants Charlotte to feel good."

"That's kind of you," Finn replied. They sat quietly, staring longingly into each other's eyes, the connection between them palpable. "I don't want to make you feel uncomfortable, but you're extraordinarily beautiful. You have the most exquisite eyes, like the color of jade," he said. Ella smiled and rested her hand in the middle of the table. Finn slowly extended his arm. He was just about to place his hand on hers when Michael burst into the room.

They both sunk back into their seats.

"Hey, guys. I didn't miss breakfast, did I?" Michael asked, dropping down into a chair beside Finn.

"DREW, WRANGLE THE EXTRAS," Jean hollered as Ella strolled onto set midday. Finn beamed at the sight of her.

Michael noticed and said, "She really is a knockout, huh?"

"Yeah," Finn mumbled.

"Before the summer is over, I've got to have her," Michael said.

"Haven't you already slept with the makeup artist and two of the extras?" Finn asked.

"Yeah, it's been a slow start," Michael joked. "Ella's special, though."

"That she is," Finn said wistfully.

Jean and Ella spoke for a moment, and then Ella hopped into his director's chair. She pulled a pen and a small notepad out of her pocket. They began shooting a scene that revolved around Finn's character making a toast to his father in honor of his birthday. Tensions were running high between the characters, with years of proverbial father-son conflict simmering barely beneath the surface. The biting toast was filled with backhanded compliments and eyes glaring instead of smiling. The other lead characters whispered amongst each other as the guests tried to maintain a facade of celebration amidst a family clearly on the verge of imploding. This pivotal scene was the first moment in the film in which this wealthy family's veneer started to lose its luster, revealing its cracks. It was obvious to Finn they were absolutely nailing it. Ella stayed for two hours, taking notes and smiling at the performers between takes. Then she walked over to Jean, nodded discreetly in Charlotte's direction, and whispered something. They hugged, and she waved goodbye to the others and left.

THEY HAD BEEN TALKING NONSTOP about the film and their plans for the next day as they enjoyed their nightly cocktails. Then Michael said, "Ella, you seemed to be taking a lot of notes today. What did you think of what you saw? How are we doing?"

"I think you're all brilliant. Don't mind my note-taking— it's just a habit." She paused to take a sip of her drink and said, "Maybe we should talk about something else. It's great to hear that everyone is feeling so inspired, though I do wonder if it would be best to remain open to the process of discovery and not do too much plodding and planning for tomorrow."

Albie smiled.

"You know what I mean," Ella said, raising her glass and clinking it to his.

"She's right. Benefit of having worked with Jean before." Albie looked at Ella and said, "You do understand what it means to create art. It can't be hammered to death."

"What do you mean?" Charlotte asked earnestly.

"The reason Jean doesn't allow blocking or rehearsals is so you'll find the moment as it's happening. There's beauty in that, truth even. As you know better than anyone, acting isn't about pretending; it's about finding what's true. You're making cinema, not a movie," Ella explained.

Jean laughed and said, "Right as always. We don't want to ruin the opportunity for spontaneity in tomorrow's shoot. I have an idea." He rubbed Ella's shoulder and continued, "Let's play one of your getting-to-know-you games."

"I love games," Michael said, leering suggestively at Ella.

Ella glanced across the table at Finn, and a subtle smile flickered across his face.

Jean explained, "Her games are marvelous. They're designed to reveal things about yourself, things you wouldn't ordinarily volunteer or even recognize. They really help a group get to know one another. After all, that's the real point of these dinners, to create intimacy that will translate on screen. Plus, it's fun to spend time together, especially when alcohol is involved." He stopped to chuckle, then added, "Once, Ella got a group of us bloody drunk and then described four different ancient perspectives on spirituality. She challenged each of us to pick and defend a position. Not the most conventional drinking game, I'd say."

"Yes, listening to you slur your answers was a real treat," Ella said, giggling.

The men laughed.

"I wouldn't be very good at something like that," Willow said nervously. "You know, a school-smart kind of thing."

Ella smiled compassionately at her. "There are all kinds of games we can play. How about this? Name four people, living or deceased, who you would like to invite over for a dinner party. There are no wrong answers."

Willow smiled and said, "That sounds fun. I guess I'd pick my mother and my grandmother; they both died when I was little. Britney Spears because I love to work out to her music. Oh, and that guy who hosts the show where people do those terrifying or gross dares. I've always had a bit of a crush on him."

Everyone smiled.

"I'm sorry you lost your mother and grandmother," Ella said.

"Yes, we're sorry," Charlotte said. The others looked on supportively.

"Thanks," Willow replied. "We were really close. I've wanted to be an entertainer for as long as I can remember. They always encouraged me to perform, even when I was little. They made costumes for me with hand-sewn sequins and entered me in all kinds of contests and pageants, cheering from the sidelines no matter what happened. Neither got to see me become successful."

"It must have been very challenging to navigate fame at such a young age when you lost two of your guiding lights," Ella said.

Willow's eyes became watery. She sniffled and said, "Yes. I felt completely lost and I craved love so badly. Along the way, wanting to be an entertainer morphed into wanting to be famous. For a long time, I thought fame was love. It really messed me up. I did a lot of stupid things trying to deal with it and trying to get a constant stream of attention because that was all I knew. I'm so embarrassed by all of it, by my past behavior. I don't want the world to see me as some kind of fallen teen star for the rest of my life. It's hard to move past that image."

Finn looked at her sympathetically. "I know it's not

the same as losing your family, and I know that it's much harder for girls and women in our industry, but I became famous as a teenager and it took me a while to get a grasp on it. I'm just glad we didn't have social media in those days. It was easier to hide from our mistakes. You're still young, and so much of your career is ahead of you. Your choices are endless."

"Thank you," Willow said.

"At some point, you realize that fame is a by-product of what we do, but it can't be the motivation. It's an illusion, not something to hang your hat on," Finn continued.

"Honestly? You don't think it's kind of great?" Michael asked. "Being adored, the special treatment . . ."

"Maybe when I was young. Now I'm just grateful to be a working actor. The rest of it is meaningless, or worse, a distraction. I try to live as privately and out of the spotlight as possible. I want to be known for the characters I portray, not my personal life."

Ella smiled warmly at him.

Finn turned to Willow and said, "You have nothing to be embarrassed about. No one gets it right when they're young, and few can understand the pressure of the spotlight, not to mention the people making millions off your labor. In the end, your talent will win out. Make the best choices you can moving forward, and don't let the past hold you back."

"Thank you. I'm trying." She paused. "Can I ask you something?"

"Sure."

"Did you ever feel like the people on your team only saw one version of you, that they clung to the image you were trying to shed?"

"How so?" Finn asked.

"Well, it's just that my manager sees me a certain way. He's always pressuring me to take jobs I don't really want."

"Don't allow anyone to pressure or pigeonhole you," Finn urged her. "Remember, he works for *you*, not the other way around. If he's not doing what you want, maybe it's time to make a change. I know it's hard to be assertive, but you have to. Your career won't survive if you let others walk all over you."

"He's managed me since I was so young. Without family, he's kind of been like a guardian. I don't know how to speak up in a way that will make him hear me. I'm not good at that. I guess it's because I'm just not that confident."

Charlotte looked at her knowingly and said, "This can be tricky for a lot of women. I've been there myself. But Finn's right—your manager should be taking direction from *you*. You're talented and more than capable of deciding what's in your best interest. You're not a child anymore."

"She's right," Ella said. She pulled a small notepad out of her pocket, flipped through the pages, and continued, "When I was taking notes today, I wrote, *Willow's performance is haunting. Subtle, yet powerful.*"

"You really wrote that?" Willow asked.

"Word for word. *You* are powerful too, perhaps more than you realize."

"Indeed," Albie said, as the others nodded in agreement.

"Thank you, all of you. I'm sorry, I didn't mean to bring the room down or make it all about me."

"Not at all," Ella assured her.

Willow took a sip of her sparkling water and said, "Charlotte, you go next. Who are your dream dinner guests?"

"Hmm. I suppose I'd pick my grandmother, William Shakespeare, Virginia Woolf, and Mary Oliver."

Jean smiled. "You have an artist's soul. It's why your performances are so sensitive and nuanced. I had been wanting to cast you for a long time. I am not disappointed."

Charlotte smiled wider than any of them had ever seen before, her fair cheeks turning rosy pink. "Thank you," she said softly, visibly grateful for the encouragement she had been longing for.

Finn and Ella exchanged a nearly imperceptible smile.

Charlotte turned to Albie and said, "You're up next."

He picked up his glass, thoughtfully swirled the bourbon before taking a sip, and slowly placed it back on the table. "It's not four people, but my answer is all of you, plus my wife. Right now, in this very moment, that's who I want to break bread with. Life is too short to waste time. That's one thing old buggers like me have on you kids. These days, I'm always exactly where I wish to be and with whom."

They sat quietly for a moment, Albie's words lingering in the air. Eventually, Jean raised his glass. "Let's drink to never wasting a moment."

"Cheers," they all said, clinking glasses.

"Finn, you're up," Albie said.

"After that? I think I'll pass for now," he replied with a chuckle. "But Albie, I do want to tell you that I'm glad you chose to do this film. It's an honor to work with you, a real dream come true. I'll always consider it a career highlight."

Albie smiled. "Likewise."

"I'll go," Michael said. "James Dean, Elvis Presley, Johnny Cash, and Marlon Brando."

"So, your idea of the perfect dinner is getting drunk with four other men? Good to know," Ella joked.

Michael turned beet red as everyone laughed.

"Okay then, who would you pick?" Michael asked, taking a swig of his drink.

"Certainly not four white men."

They all laughed even harder. Charlotte had to cover her mouth with her hand.

"My answer would change daily, but for today I'll say Colette, Jean-Michel Basquiat, Simone de Beauvoir, and Mary Magdalene," Ella replied.

Finn smiled so widely, it caught everyone's attention. Ella raised an eyebrow and said, "What are you thinking?"

"It's just such a great answer. You want to be around people who innovate—artists, creators, and thinkers."

She smiled. "Of course. That's why I'm here with all of you."

CHARLOTTE WAS THE FIRST TO EXCUSE herself to her room, followed shortly by Michael and Willow, who wanted to speak privately about a scene they were working on later that week. Jean finished his drink and announced, "Well, I'm heading up. I have some details for tomorrow to obsess over."

"Always the artist," Ella said. "Or a lunatic, perhaps."

Jean chuckled and kissed her on each cheek.

Albie grabbed the bottle that the waiter had left on the table and poured himself another three fingers of bourbon. He held the bottle up to offer the others a refill.

"No, thank you," Ella replied.

Finn shook his head.

"Albie, are you all right? You've had quite a lot to drink tonight," Ella said.

"I'm fine. No need to worry about an old-timer like me. I'll finish this and head off to dreamland."

"I can stay and walk up with you," Finn offered.

"I'm okay. Get some sleep. With my wrinkled face, no one will notice the bags under my eyes, but you're still a leading man," Albie replied.

Finn chuckled.

Ella walked over and pecked Albie on the cheek. "Do get some rest, my friend. Good night."

"I'll walk you up," Finn said.

She smiled, and they headed upstairs together.

"You seem worried about him. I can pop back down in a bit and make sure he's okay," Finn offered.

"That's sweet of you. Get some sleep—you're filming tomorrow. It's just that Albie and I go way back. There's something going on with him. His answer to my silly game was so kind and sentimental. He's usually such a crusty old bird."

Finn laughed.

"The heavy drinking concerns me too. He gave that up years ago, or at least I thought he had."

"I'll keep an eye on him," Finn said.

She smiled.

"Did you see Charlotte's face when Jean complimented her tonight?" he asked. "I know that was because of whatever you said to him."

"I was glad to. He has a good heart; he sometimes just needs a nudge in the right direction." She paused and added, "You were truly kind to Willow. Your words meant a lot to her. She needs that kind of encouragement and compassion until she finds her way."

"It was my pleasure," he said, smiling.

"You're a good person, Finn Forrester."

He blushed.

Finn realized they were standing outside of Ella's room. They stood facing each other, so close they were practically touching. After a long, electric moment had passed, Ella said, "This is me. I should probably turn in. Have a good night."

"You too, Ella," he said, turning to leave.

She put her key in the door and pushed it open. Before stepping inside, she glanced over at Finn puttering down the hallway. He felt her gaze and turned around. They made eye contact, exchanged a smile, and she disappeared into her room.

 **CHAPTER 6**

Finn bounded into the dining room the next morning to see a familiar sight: Albie tucked in the corner and Ella sitting at what had become their usual table. "I beat you," she said, smiling brightly. She was wearing a long, flowing lavender sundress, her hair falling freely around her shoulders.

"You look beautiful," he said as he took the seat opposite her.

She glanced down, blushing.

"Am I making you uncomfortable?"

"No, not in the least." She looked into his eyes and said, "It's not every day a handsome movie star pays me a compliment."

He smiled bashfully. "So, you think I'm handsome?"

"Incredibly."

He reached his hand across the table, but before he could make contact, the waiter came barreling over with a pot of coffee. Finn pulled his hand back and said, "Thank you," as the waiter poured his dark roast.

"Would you like something to eat, Miss Sinclair? The usual?" the waiter asked.

"My usual, please," Ella replied.

"Likewise, and thank you," Finn said. The waiter darted off, and Finn directed his attention back to Ella. "So, you were saying that you think I'm irresistible."

She giggled.

"I'm just kidding," he said with a laugh.

"You are certainly a movie star. Tell me, what inspired you to become an actor?"

"It's the only thing I ever wanted to do. Truthfully, I never considered doing anything else. It never felt like much of a choice, more like a dream or a calling."

"And you went for it. That's brave."

He smiled. "I was lucky to grow up in LA. My mother only worked part-time, so she was able to drive me all over the place. I started auditioning when I was a kid. Did my first play when I was ten. As they say, I was bitten. A couple of commercials followed, and then when I was a teenager, movies featuring high school and college kids became the fad. It was lucky timing. One director cast me in a few things, and sure enough, I had a string of successful movies under my belt before the age of twenty. Having that kind of success early on opened a lot of doors; of course, I didn't fully understand at the time that things don't often go that way. I'm extremely fortunate."

"It was obviously meant to be. I've seen many of your films. You're enormously talented. There's always such depth and sensitivity to your work, no matter the role. You're a gifted performer."

"Thank you," he said, blushing. "I'm flattered."

"What's your process like? How do you approach your characters? I know Charlotte is trained as a method actor, although with Jean's insistence on nighttime socializing, I'm sure she's had to adjust her process."

"That's a great question. I've never been one for method acting. It works for some people, like Charlotte, but there's a price to pay for identifying so closely with a role. I've never wanted my work to take over my life, so I try to develop my characters in a way that still allows me to step in and out of the role. For me, that's part of the skill of acting. Usually, I begin by creating a backstory beyond the script, trying to get to know him—his motivations, emotional center, mannerisms. Naturally, you discover more things as you go and see what works when you're trying it out with other actors, the director, the cinematographer. That's part of the fun of it all. The collaboration. The group storytelling. In the end, though, I take responsibility for my performance."

"Is it easier when you like the character? You must have your choice of projects. How do you decide between scripts?"

"Once in a blue moon, something like this comes along with a filmmaker or director I've always wanted to work with, but typically, it's about the story. I'm less concerned with my own character. For better or worse, I've taken on unflattering roles because they were integral to the bigger picture. The best characters aren't wholly good or bad, but when I've portrayed someone truly reprehensible, yes, it's challenging. When there's nothing I can identify with, I have to approach it differently. I'm not frightened by that, though. When I receive a script, I ask myself: What's the story? What's the message? I try to be a part of telling stories that ought to be told, if that makes sense."

"Perfect sense," she replied with a grin. "I've spent quite a bit of time with actors, and I've learned there are two types."

"Do tell."

"Well, there are those who focus on their role. You know, if it's a big part, a juicy part, something that could score them some industry gold, make them a standout. Then there are the others, the true artists and storytellers who understand they are part of something larger. They understand that it's not really about them. You're in that group."

He smiled. "That's kind of you."

Just then, Michael came vaulting into the room.

"Ah, and there's the other type," Ella said quietly.

Finn burst into laughter.

"Good morning, guys," Michael said as he sat down. "What's so funny?"

ELLA MADE IT TO THE SHOOT IN THE early afternoon and bumped into the actors walking back to set from their trailers. "Hey, guys," she said.

"We were just heading back from our lunch break while the crew sets up for the next scene," Finn said. He noticed her hands and asked, "Leaky pen?"

She glanced down at her hands stained with blue and giggled. "I went berry picking. Perfect day for it. How's it been going on set today?"

"Fine," Charlotte replied. "So far, we've just been capturing some of the small talk for the party scene, but Albie and Willow have a big scene coming up next. The rest of us will get a break as we mingle in the background."

Ella looked over at Willow, who was fidgeting nervously. They smiled at one another as they made their way into the ballroom. Jean and Drew were huddled together, so the actors stood on the sidelines waiting for instructions. Ella approached Albie, leaned in, and whispered, "You're a legend, dear friend. Must be quite daunting for a young actor to go toe to toe with you."

Albie glanced over at Willow, who was taking considered breaths, clearly trying to calm her nerves. He squeezed Ella's hand and winked at her.

"Places, everyone!" Jean hollered.

The actors scattered to hit their marks, and Ella hopped into Jean's director's chair. Jean approached Albie and Willow. "This is meant to be an intimate moment. When you two are dancing, it's not just about the conversation. The magic of the scene will be in your expressions and the way you look at one another. Willow, your character has a pure heart. She's not jaded like the others, although they've wounded her deeply. That needs to come through, despite the minimal dialogue. It's all in your face. Make yourself vulnerable. Keep it honest."

Albie squeezed Willow's hand and smiled, and Jean headed over to Ella.

"Rolling . . . Action!"

Albie took Willow's hand and said, "May I have a dance with my darling girl?"

"Sure, Daddy."

He took her hand in his, and she placed her other hand on his shoulder. They began to sway to the music, partygoers waltzing around them. She smiled sweetly, looking at him with love. "The staff really outdid themselves tonight. Everything is so beautiful. Are you enjoying your party?"

"I suppose. Not as much as your husband, though," he said, glancing over to the bar. "Looks like he's three sheets to the wind already."

"Daddy, please . . ." she muttered, averting her eyes in shame.

"I'm sorry. I know things are a bit tense. I just want to make sure you're happy. Life is short, and you deserve the best."

She looked at him innocently and said, "How do we really know what any of us deserves?"

He took a moment, gazing at her adoringly, pondering her question. "How did I get so lucky to have you? You couldn't be more different from your entitled, self-absorbed brother. He's mad as hell that I won't step down and name him as my successor, as if I'm already one foot in the grave. Glares at me every chance he gets. Perhaps I should watch my drink around him."

"At least he doesn't call you illegitimate," she said with a sorrowful look.

He furrowed his brow.

"I overheard him talking to some people earlier. That's how he referred to me," she said. "It's okay, I'm used to it."

"My dear, sweet girl, there is nothing illegitimate about you. While my relationship with your mother was brief, it was one of the best things I've ever done. You are the most glorious blessing in my life. I couldn't be prouder of you. Your brother is just jealous." He lowered his voice and continued, "Between us, you're the only one in this room who truly brings me joy. Never forget that."

A soft smile swept across her face, her eyes sparkling. She rested her cheek on his shoulder and whispered, "I love you, Daddy."

"Cut!" Jean called.

The entire room fell silent.

Willow looked around nervously. All at once, the entire cast and crew erupted in applause.

"Well done," Albie said, squeezing her hands.

"That was so lovely," Charlotte said.

"That was one of the most beautiful scenes I've ever witnessed," Finn added. "Your faces spoke volumes."

"I was just playing off of Willow's gorgeous performance," Albie said.

Jean hustled over. "You nailed it. At the end, when you put your head on his shoulder . . ."

"I know it wasn't in the script. I can do it differently next time," Willow said sheepishly.

"*Non, ma chérie*. It was perfect," Jean assured her. "We're going to run it again to capture it from another angle."

As soon as Jean dashed off, Albie leaned close to Willow and Ella heard him whisper, "When I said there is nothing illegitimate about you, I wasn't only thinking of your character. Willow, there is *nothing* illegitimate about you. You have earned your spot here. Don't forget that."

Willow smiled brightly.

"Places, everyone," Jean yelled. "Rolling . . . Action!"

AS THE DINNER DISHES WERE CLEARED that night, the waiter turned to Ella and asked, "Shall we bring dessert now?"

"Please do," she replied. She turned to Albie. "So, were you going to tell us it's your birthday?"

"Oh, bugger," Albie groaned. "Isn't it enough that we've been celebrating my character's birthday for weeks?"

"No, it most certainly is not," Ella replied.

"Happy birthday, old friend," Jean said.

"Happy birthday," they all echoed, surprise on their faces.

"How old?" Jean asked.

"Seventy-four," Albie replied. He turned to Ella. "You never forget a bloody thing, do you?"

She smiled. "Life should be celebrated. After all, isn't that what you're all here making a film about? You're an extraordinary artist and a dear friend; naturally we want to mark the occasion of your birthday."

"I would tell you that I'm just an old bag of bones and to save your energy, but I know it would be pointless," Albie replied.

"That it would be," Ella agreed. "Besides, you can't fool us. Many men would willingly trade years of their life for the chance to live one day as Albie Hughes. I suspect it's a fair trade." She leaned closer to him, lowered her voice, and said, "You have more zest for life than many men half your age. You always have. Even if you are a stubborn old goat."

Everyone laughed.

"All right, if you're all so desperate for cake, I'll play along. I guess you only live once," Albie said.

Ella shook her head. "No, my dear friend. You only die once. You live every day, every moment."

Albie let out a puff and smiled. "You are a good friend, Ella. Wise beyond your years."

The waiter came in carrying a tray with a homemade blueberry tart with a single candle. Ella began singing "Happy Birthday," and everyone joined in. Albie's face turned red. He stared at the candle, lost in thought.

"You sure you have enough oxygen left in those prehistoric lungs to blow that out?" Ella joked.

Albie laughed, inhaled deeply, and blew out the candle. Everyone applauded. The waiter took the tart back to the kitchen to prepare servings.

"I hope you made a good wish," Ella said.

"Indeed, I did. I can't believe you had them make a blueberry tart."

"I remembered it was your favorite," Ella replied. "Picked the berries myself this morning. Wild blueberries are the best. Lucky for us, they're in season. The kitchen was kind enough to make a delicious-looking tart." She paused and said, "Albie, tell them about how you met Margaret. It's such a wonderful story. I'm sure everyone would love to hear it."

"I would," Finn said, as he and Ella exchanged a smile.

"Me too," Charlotte added. "In the many years we've known each other, I don't think I've ever heard this story."

Albie smiled. "All right," he said. The waitstaff returned and passed around plates, each with a slice of tart and generous dollop of freshly made whipped cream.

They all started eating and Albie began, "I met her at a party in London thrown by some aristocrat. Completely pretentious. I was the lead in a play on the West End, and the director invited me. You know how that blue-blooded set loves to have a celebrity in their midst, something to gab about when they're at their holiday homes."

Everyone laughed.

Albie took a bite of his tart and continued, "I brought a girl with me, some actress, can't even remember her name. We were all dressed in absurdly formal attire, could hardly tell the guests from the waitstaff, eating catered, crustless watercress sandwiches or some such rubbish. All of a sudden, in walks a stunningly beautiful woman wearing a simple, sky-blue frock and holding a pie. It's hard to overstate how extraordinarily out of place she looked. I was immediately transfixed. She had the biggest, most beautiful eyes, and her hair fell in waves." He paused, as if reliving every detail. "Anyway, the host's wife ran over, greeted her, and ferried the pie over to the dessert table. I couldn't take my eyes off this woman. The way she moved, her smile, the way her eyes sparkled when she laughed. I watched her for hours. I asked someone about her, and they said she was an elementary school teacher who happened to know the sister of the host. Eventually, I saw her standing alone at the dessert table and decided to make my move. The table was covered in mile-high meringues and fancy chocolate tortes encased in sugar domes, no doubt from the finest bakery in London, and there was her humble homemade pie off to the side. I sidled up to her and said, 'Everything looks good.' She smiled at me, and I felt like I was struck by lightning. I picked up a plate and a serving utensil and said, 'I think I'm going to try this one,' and I took a slice of the blueberry pie. She looked at me and said, 'I made that. To tell you the truth, I feel like a bit of a fool. I didn't know what kind of party it was.' I said, 'I'm Albie, what's your name?' In her angelic voice, she said, 'Margaret.' I'll tell you, I fell completely in love with her then and there."

"What about your date?" Michael asked.

"Broke up with her at the party. I called a car for her and sent her home. Felt terrible about it, but when you meet the one, you can't let anything stand in your way. True love is the greatest gift in the world; one mustn't squander it or be foolish enough to think it will simply wait until it obliges our schedules."

"So, it really was love at first sight," Charlotte said wistfully.

"Indeed. Anyone who tells you that love at first sight isn't real, well, those unlucky bastards have just never experienced it. Take it from an old fucker like me: when you get hit by lightning, you surrender to it. All the details, the little things you don't know about each other, you'll learn those over time, and if you really love each other, most of it won't matter. There's no replacing that inexplicable, inconvenient, all-encompassing feeling of love. Standing there in that moment, holding that slice of pie, I knew I couldn't live without her. These days, people court each other like they're applying for a job or running through a checklist. But this is where the artists—the poets, the novelists, the filmmakers— have always known better: true love has no reason."

"How long have you two been married?" Finn asked.

"We celebrated our fortieth anniversary a few months ago."

"Wow," Finn muttered.

"I told you it was a great story," Ella said, catching Finn's eye. They stared at each other for a moment.

"Some people say romantic love fades over time," Charlotte said.

"Rubbish!" Albie replied fervently. "It changes, yes. In

many ways, it grows. But I'll tell you this much: the first time we slept together was the most earth-shattering experience of my life. Still is, when I can convince her to do it."

They all laughed.

"Needless to say, blueberry pie has been my favorite dessert ever since. Mmm, that was scrumptious. Thank you, Ella," Albie said, scraping the last bite of tart off his plate. He picked up his glass and took a healthy swig of bourbon to wash it down.

"Since you've been such a good sport about dessert, I'm hoping you'll indulge us a bit more. What's a party without dancing?" Ella said, rising. She set up her phone to play music through the speaker on the bar. "I think we could all use a whirl around the dance floor. Albie, I know I'm no substitute for your Margaret, but I'd love the first dance with you."

He chuckled. "If a gorgeous young thing like you wants to dance with me, who am I to say no?"

"Good, I know just the song," she called as Rod Stewart's "Maggie May" came swirling into the room.

Albie laughed and rose to take her hand.

"Come on, everyone," she said, turning to the others. "This is a party!"

"I'll sit and watch." Jean raised his glass. "You all have fun."

"Come on, movie wife," Michael said to Willow.

"Looks like it's us," Finn told Charlotte.

The three couples danced around the room, smiling and laughing. As the next song came on, Charlotte turned to Albie and said, "I'd like a spin with the guest of honor."

"With pleasure," he replied, taking her hand.

Finn looked at Ella, but Michael swooped in and said, "Dance with me," dragging her to the dance floor before she could respond.

She glanced over at Finn and then twirled away with Michael.

A FEW SONGS LATER, FINN DANCED with Willow but couldn't stop watching Michael pulling Ella's body against his and whispering in her ear. At one point, she glanced over with a "save me" look in her eyes. He smiled. When the song ended, Finn walked over and said, "I'm cutting in for the next one, if Ella will have me."

"Suit yourself," Michael replied with a shrug. "Charlotte, let's give it a go."

Finn looked at Ella longingly and asked, "May I?"

"Please, I've been waiting," she replied, smiling warmly.

"Me too."

He gently took her hand and placed his other hand on the small of her back. They each inhaled deeply at their first touch. She rested her hand on his shoulder, pulled him close, and they started to sway, staring at each other as though there were no one else in the room. Their bodies fit together as if they were built to belong.

"I love this song," she said.

"What is it?" he asked.

"It's a love song called 'Amalfi.' She's singing about a man she fell for. They couldn't be together because they both had other things they needed to do in the world, but they're together now. She compares his beauty to the Amalfi Coast."

Finn smiled. "Love really inspires people. Listening to Albie talk about his wife, wow."

"Have you ever felt that way about someone?" she asked.

"When I was twenty, I had someone special. Maybe it was love. She died young. Devastated me."

"I'm so sorry."

"I've had relationships in the years since, but I can't

call any of them true love. It's why I haven't married, even though I've longed to share my life with someone. I've always felt that someday I'd meet a woman who would knock me off my feet, and I'd know with certainty she's the one, the one I don't want to live without. What about you?"

She shook her head. "Just a lot of short-lived romances, the kind of affairs that aren't meant to last. I've had a knack for meeting the wrong guy. Or maybe I've been the wrong girl. There's been no one I've wanted to . . ."

"What?" he asked softly.

"Give everything to."

He took a deep breath. "Ella, you're exquisite. If you ever give yourself completely to someone, he'll be the luckiest man on the planet."

"Finn, I . . ."

Before she could finish, an up-tempo song came on and Michael hollered, "Everyone, group dance time! Jean, jump up and join us."

"Uh, thank you for the dance," Ella said as she pulled away from Finn.

He smiled faintly. She took his hand and gently squeezed it. "Ella," he said softly, but Willow grabbed Ella's arm and pulled her over to the group, and he missed his chance.

"Gosh, you and Finn look like you're a couple or something," Willow commented innocently over the music. "You look so good together."

Ella and Finn exchanged a look, and they all danced into the wee hours of the night.

One by one, they excused themselves and retired for the evening. Soon, only Ella, Finn, and Jean remained. Eventually, even Jean said, "I'm going upstairs. Your manuscripts are waiting for me."

"And I bet I know which one you'll start with," Ella joked.

Jean kissed her on each cheek, said, "*Bonsoir*," and left.

Ella and Finn sat for a moment, gazing at each other. "Well, I should probably get some sleep, and you're filming tomorrow," Ella said.

"May I walk you up?" Finn asked.

She smiled and they headed upstairs.

"It was so sweet of you to plan this evening for Albie," Finn said.

"I was glad to. Good things should be celebrated. Since I first heard the story of how he met Margaret, blueberries have reminded me of love, epic love. Can't eat one without thinking that they taste like love." She giggled.

"I don't think I'll ever eat another blueberry again without thinking the same."

After a long pause, as their eyes lingered on one another, Ella said, "Anyway, I've gotten to know Albie over the years, mostly through Jean. I've always had a bit of a soft spot for him."

"He clearly has one for you too. He's a legend to guys like me. He's had a hell of a career on both stage and screen, and I've admired him for a long time. It's been a dream to work with him, to get to know him."

"It was nice that you told him so the other night. Sometimes, I think . . ."

"What?" he asked, staring into her eyes.

"Just that we don't tell people what they mean to us when we have the chance."

Finn took a breath. "Sometimes we want to, more than anything, but we're not sure if they're ready to hear it."

Finn's words hung in the air between them as they stood outside of Ella's room, so close they were practically touching. After a long moment passed, Ella said, "Here we are. Thank you again for the dance."

"It was absolutely my pleasure."

"Have a good night."

"You too," he said, turning to leave.

She stuck her key in the door, and Finn delicately put his hand on her wrist to stop her. She turned to look at him, sparks flying between them.

"Breakfast tomorrow?" he asked. "We could try eating a little earlier so we can be alone."

She smiled. "Sure, I'd love to. See you in the morning. Good night."

"Good night."

 **CHAPTER 7**

Bright and early the next morning, Finn walked into the dining room, looking for Ella. To his surprise, he instead saw Jean and Albie having breakfast together at the large table they shared each night for dinner. "Finn, join us," Jean called.

"Good morning," Finn said as he sat down, noticing dark circles under Jean's bloodshot eyes. There was a typed manuscript spread out on the table, the pages marked with red ink.

Jean signaled to the waiter. "Another espresso."

"Coffee, please," Finn said.

"More water for your tea?" the waiter asked Albie.

He nodded.

"I'm surprised to see you here," Finn remarked.

"I barely slept last night. Ella gave me the manuscript for her philosophical treatise on sex. I made the mistake of starting it, and I couldn't put the damn thing down. I was up half the night reading it and then spent the other half obsessing about it," he explained, swallowing the last dregs of espresso. "You wouldn't believe some of the things in here," he said, shuffling through the papers and pushing them into a messy pile.

"That Ella is really something," Albie said with a soft smile. "There's precious little I would give up my alone time in the morning for, but Jean read me some excerpts and I'm hooked. Riveting stuff. Very provocative." He chuckled. "She's quite a woman."

Just then, Michael strutted into the room, quickly scanning it. He looked taken aback to see all the men sitting together. He joined them just as the waiter delivered their drinks.

"I'll have an espresso," Michael said.

"Would anyone like something to eat?"

"Not yet," Finn replied. "Thank you."

"Well, this isn't what I was expecting this morning," Michael said. "All that's missing are the women. Where are they?" he asked, glancing around the room. It was clear he was looking for Ella, since the others never had breakfast in the dining room.

Jean ignored him and said, "Fascinating, just fascinating," as he flipped through the manuscript. "I can't stop thinking about it."

"What'd I miss?" Michael asked as his espresso was delivered.

"It's Ella's book about sex. I was up all night with it. You wouldn't believe some of the things she wrote. Here," Jean said, pulling out several pages. "She has eight pages in a row about thrusting."

Michael's and Finn's eyes widened, their mouths agape.

"I told you it's provocative," Albie said with a sly laugh as he picked up his tea and took a measured sip.

Jean continued, "She describes thirteen different ways men thrust when they have sexual intercourse, in *great* detail, and what each method signifies about their feelings toward their partner and the type of pleasure they are trying to elicit for themselves. She calls the section 'Thirteen

Thrusts.'" He looked at them and said, "I swear! That's what she calls it!"

"Does she have like a favorite or a recommendation or anything?" Michael asked.

Finn shot him a disapproving look while Albie laughed.

"What? I'm obviously not implying I need help in that department, but I am definitely curious. You know, a woman's perspective and all," Michael said defensively.

"It's not meant to be a diary or how-to guide," Jean said. "It's rather brilliant, actually. Her ideas are bold. Americans can be quite puritanical about sex. She just loves pushing people past their comfort zones. Of course, like all her work, it's gorgeously written. There are some incredibly funny bits." He stopped to chuckle. "She has the most wonderful sense of humor, especially when writing about taboo subjects."

"It is quite tantalizing. Tell them what she wrote about blow jobs," Albie said with a mischievous glint in his eyes.

"Yes, you simply must hear this," Jean said, searching through the manuscript.

Just then, Ella walked in wearing a black sundress and sandals, the chains hanging around her neck tinkling like wind chimes as she moved. Everyone turned to look. She cocked her head and furrowed her brow in confusion as she approached the table of men who were all smiling broadly.

"Well, good morning," she said. "This is unexpected." She and Finn exchanged a covert look as Jean scooched over to make room for her. She plopped down and asked, "So, how is everyone this fine morning?"

"I was just telling them about your book," Jean replied. "Bloody thing kept me up all night."

"That explains why you look a fright," she observed.

"We must discuss your description of the erect cock."

Michael had just taken a sip of espresso, which went flying out of his mouth. He grabbed a napkin to wipe it up. Finn's faced turned bright red.

"Gee, give a girl a minute to wake up. I haven't even had a cup of tea," Ella casually replied.

Jean hollered at the waiter, "Tea!" and he pointed to Ella. He continued, "I'm serious, *ma chérie*. I'm utterly possessed thinking of it. Your description of hardness and thrusting on page thirty-eight is haunting."

She giggled. "I'm barely awake, Jean. Perhaps you could take it down a notch with the cock talk."

Finn and Albie laughed.

"I don't know how I'm going to concentrate on filming today. You've got my mind spinning. All I want to do is discuss blow jobs," Jean said.

"And you wonder why Charlotte and Willow never come to breakfast," Ella joked.

Finn cracked up.

"I'm serious," Jean said. "It's captivating."

"Perhaps you shouldn't have read the whole thing in one go. Swallowed more than you could handle, as it were. I warned you there's adult subject matter," she jested.

Finn, Albie, and Michael tried to muffle their laughter.

"Do you think that what you wrote about the half-hard, pity thrust is true? Do other women feel this way?" Jean asked.

"I don't know. Let's ask one of your three ex-wives," she joked.

Everyone burst into laughter. Albie nearly fell off his chair. The waiter delivered Ella's tea and asked, "Would anyone like breakfast?"

"We waited for you," Finn said.

Ella smiled. "A soft-boiled egg and some fruit, please."

"Same for me," Michael said, winking at her.

"Oatmeal and berries, please," Finn said.

Jean and Albie, having already eaten, shook their heads.

As soon as the waiter walked away, Jean handed her the manuscript and said, "I made some notes in the margins."

"Thank you," she replied. "You're a good friend, lascivious though you may be."

"The vignette about slut shaming was hysterical. I laughed out loud. Oh, but the funniest section was the part about group sex," Jean said.

"Group sex?" Michael asked, his eyes like saucers.

"It's very clever," Jean said. "She wrote it as a scene in a satirical screenplay. At first, the director tries to give gentle, appropriate notes, but by the end he's barking out vulgarities and ordering them to do outrageous things all while insisting they mind the camera. It's wickedly funny."

Ella giggled. "I thought you'd appreciate that."

"So, Ella," Michael said, his eyes fixed on her, "what made you interested in writing about sex?"

"She theorizes about pleasure. It's not done in an effort to be scandalous or salacious. It's intelligent," Finn said. He glanced at Ella, who was smiling at him with her eyes. "She's interested in things that people experience with a oneness or wholeness. Sex is just one topic. She also writes about art, food, and nature; she explores fundamental questions about how we as human beings experience pleasure, and by extension, how we may arrive at the true feelings of joy, peace, and belonging that so often elude us. Or so I imagine."

Ella smiled softly. "Yes, that's right. At least, it's what I'm attempting to do."

"Well, I can't wait to read it," Michael said. "It sounds, uh, enlightening."

The waiter delivered their breakfast, and the conversation moved on while they ate. Eventually, Jean said, "We should all head to set. Ella, would you like to join us?"

She shook her head. "I'm going to have more tea and catch up on some work. I'll pop by later."

He pecked her on each cheek and said, "*Brava, ma chérie.* It's a wonderful book. With any luck, I'll be able to get it out of my mind and focus on the damn shoot."

She giggled.

The four men all said goodbye and left. A moment later, Finn darted back into the room.

"Hey," she said softly, surprised to see him.

"Hey. I told them I forgot something, and they're holding the van for me. I'm sorry about breakfast this morning. I was hoping to spend some time alone with you. I had no idea they'd all be here."

"That's okay. It's my fault. I should've known I'd get an earful from Jean when he read the book. Figures he started with that one and not the one about art." She rolled her eyes playfully.

Finn smiled. "After dinner tonight, will you take that walk around the grounds with me?"

"I'd love to."

"I really have to go," he said. "Have a great day."

"You too. Break a leg."

THE VAN DROPPED ELLA AT THE SET just before noon. On her way inside, she saw Willow walking to her trailer and stopped to say hello.

"How's it going today?" Ella asked.

"Fine, I think. It's always so hard to tell with him, although we all have a better handle on things now. I think it's starting to come together."

"That's great," Ella said. "It's a process. Jean always films so much more than he needs. Don't worry, he'll find the moments that sparkle and string them together into a beautiful story."

"I couldn't believe it when my manager told me he wanted me for this film. It's not exactly the kind of thing I'm typically offered—you know, I'm usually asked to be the half-naked girl running and screaming in a horror film, or the coked-out love interest of some interesting male character." She paused. "I was really nervous when we started. I had awful anxiety each time I was called to set. I've had more panic attacks here than I've ever had before. The other actors are so much more experienced than I am. I was worried that I wouldn't be able to keep up and that they'd all wonder why I was even cast. I'm not exactly in the same league."

Ella smiled warmly at her. "Jean sees something in you, even if you can't see it yet. He's never wrong about these things. You deserve to be here just as much as the others. Trust that. You certainly proved yourself yesterday. Don't let anyone intimidate you, not even Jean."

"Thank you. Everyone was so sweet and supportive yesterday. Albie really encouraged me. He took me seriously, you know?"

"That's because he knows you're talented. You have a natural gift. It's clear to everyone."

Willow blushed. "The shoot has been a lot more fun since you got here. Everyone loves having you around."

"That's sweet."

"Finn can't stop talking about you. I guess Jean read your book or something; the guys were all blabbing on and on about it. Charlotte's dying to read it. She's a big fan of yours. Finn was saying the nicest things, about how smart you are, how talented, how beautiful. He thinks you're brilliant. It must be nice to have a guy see you that way."

Ella smiled. "Where are you off to?"

"Charlotte and Finn are working on a scene. My character is out of frame, so I'm going to hang out in my trailer and prep for my next scene. Michael isn't on camera either, but he stayed to watch. See you back at the inn tonight?"

"Sure. See you later."

Ella strolled onto set while they were between takes. Finn noticed her immediately, smiled, and nodded his hello.

She smiled in return and waved hello to Charlotte, Michael, and Albie.

"Darling, I'm glad you're here," Jean said, dashing over to her. "We're trying to capture a quiet, intimate moment in the middle of this colossal party, and you know how delicate that can be. Please, stay and watch."

She nodded.

"Everyone in position," Jean hollered. "Rolling . . . Action!"

Finn and Charlotte exchanged some brief dialogue, then he placed his hand gently on her cheek and they kissed.

"Cut," Jean hollered.

Finn immediately looked over at Ella, a pained expression on his face as if to say he was sorry.

"Again," Jean called. "Places, everyone. Rolling . . . Action!"

This time as Finn placed his hand on Charlotte's face, he looked past her, directly at Ella, and then kissed her.

"Cut," Jean called. "That was better. There was much more feeling. Again. Places."

They shot another dozen takes. Each time, Finn looked at Ella as he touched Charlotte. After watching the scene fourteen times, Ella whispered to Jean, "I have to go."

"Darling, stay longer."

"Don't worry. You've gotten what you're after. It's incredibly intimate. Hauntingly so."

As Ella walked off set, she turned and noticed Finn watching her with a troubled look on his face. Michael looked like he was about to follow her outside, so she scurried away as Jean called, "Places, everyone. Rolling . . . Action!"

"Ella!" Michael called as she was traipsing to the van. She stopped, turned to him, and said, "Hey."

"Did you have enough already? You didn't see any of my scenes today."

"Another day," she said politely.

"They'll probably be working on that bit between Finn and Charlotte for a while anyway. Perk of being an actor, I suppose—being paid boatloads of money to make out with attractive people."

"It's just acting," she said. "Hardly as intimate as kissing when there isn't a camera crew and room full of extras watching."

"You're right about that. It's so much better with privacy," he said, looking at her suggestively. "It would still bother me if I were Charlotte's husband or Finn's girlfriend, though. It's why I never let myself get tied down—too much drama explaining this kind of stuff to people you're dating. Better to keep things casual."

"Did you say Finn has a girlfriend?"

"Oh yeah, they've been together for a couple of years. She wants to marry him. He told me about her when we first got here."

Ella looked away.

"Listen, I'm heading to my trailer until they call for me. Come, hang out. I'd love to hear more about your book. It sounds riveting."

"Sorry, I have work to do. I'll see you later."

"You'll be at dinner?" he asked.

"Wouldn't miss it."

AT THE END OF THE DAY'S SHOOT, the actors were all heading to their trailers to change into their street clothes before going back to the inn. Jean called to Finn, "Stay behind for a minute."

Finn walked over and said, "I felt good today, like we were on to it. I can do it differently tomorrow if you prefer. Are you getting what you want?"

"Yes, we captured some gorgeous moments. It's not about the film. There's a personal matter I wish to discuss."

Finn looked at him expectantly.

"It's about Ella," Jean said.

Finn took a breath and looked down.

"You are in love with her."

"Jean, nothing has happened. I . . ."

Jean shook his head. "I see the way you look at her. I noticed it the first night she arrived, and every moment since, your eyes have betrayed you. Of course, I've seen many men become infatuated with Ella, most of whom she has no interest in. The connection runs much deeper with you. The way you spoke about her work this morning. The look on your face when you had to kiss Charlotte in front of her. Don't try to deny it. You're not *that* good an actor."

Finn exhaled and his shoulders slumped. "She's an extraordinary woman. I've never met anyone like her. I think we have a connection. But I'm completely committed to this film, so if . . ."

"It's all right. She is not my lover. You are both adults. I didn't want you to feel as though you must sneak around."

"Thank you. I appreciate that."

"You are right that she is an extraordinary woman. If she returns your affection, you're a lucky man." He paused and added, "Perhaps it isn't my place, but there is something you should know."

"I'm listening."

"Ella may be unattainable. Yes, she is a romantic and a free spirit, but I've never seen her give herself fully to any man. I'm not certain she ever will. I've always suspected she intentionally dates men she'll never love." He huffed before continuing, "But I've seen the way she looks at you, so perhaps there's a first time for everything. Besides, I suspect you're so far gone that you'll take your chances. Good luck, *mon ami.*"

"I WONDER WHERE ELLA IS," Willow said. Everyone had been nursing their first round of drinks for over twenty minutes and the buffet was open, but Ella hadn't shown up.

"We spoke for a little while today as she was leaving the set. She said she'd be at dinner," Michael said.

"Maybe she's immersed in her book project," Charlotte suggested. "My husband always loses track when he's working on a play. Time rarely means much to writers."

"That's the truth," Jean agreed. "Ruined my second marriage. One night, my wife confronted me in the middle of the night when I was banging away on a script. She said, 'Would you rather fuck me or finish that fucking script?' I chose the script."

Everyone laughed.

"You're a real artist. I could never pick work over sex," Michael said.

"He didn't. He was sleeping with their cleaning woman, Vivienne, who no doubt serviced him as he worked," Ella said as she flitted into the room.

Finn turned to look at her, but she headed straight for Jean, sliding into the booth next to him. "For all we know, she was tending to his needs under the desk at the very moment his wife was screaming at him."

Albie laughed so hard that it morphed into a cackle.

"That's the trouble with old friends—they know all your secrets," Jean said, squeezing Ella's shoulders. "Of course, she's right. I couldn't get my wife out of the room fast enough. Vivienne was a generous, sensual woman. Terrible cleaner, though. Broke nearly every vase and piece of crystal in the house."

The room exploded with laughter.

"Sex uncomplicated by feelings. Is that your holy grail?" Ella asked.

Jean shrugged. "Sexual energy clutters the mind. One needs to get a good dusting to be creative. I am an artist, after all."

Ella crinkled her nose and smiled. "At least you embrace who you are. Can't fault you for that. It's honest."

"Speaking of honest, there's so much more I want to discuss about your book," Jean said.

"Oh please, not tonight, Jean. I've had more than enough sex talk today. Read the book on art when you have the chance, and then we'll chat more. I'd like to give them both to Charlotte as well, if she'd like to read them."

Charlotte smiled brightly. "I would be honored. I admire your work enormously."

"You're such a talented artist," Ella said. "I don't want to impose, but I'd be delighted to hear your feedback, if you have any time to spare while we're all here."

"I'll make time," Charlotte replied.

"Shall we eat?" Jean asked.

"We waited for you," Finn said, looking at Ella. "We were wondering if everything was okay."

She wouldn't meet his eyes and kept her body turned slightly away from him. "Lost track of time. Sorry to hold everyone up. You should have gone on without me."

"Nonsense. We're not on a bloody schedule," Albie said, taking a swig of his bourbon.

"It's more fun with you here," Willow said sweetly.

Ella turned to her and smiled.

"Jean's right about sexual energy. I got a little, uh, *exercise* today with one of the extras, and I'm famished," Michael said, springing to his feet to get dinner. The others slowly followed. Finn and Ella found themselves the last two at the buffet again. Finn desperately tried to make eye contact with her, but her gaze was singularly focused on the selection of food.

"Ella, is everything okay?" he asked softly.

"Uh-huh."

"You haven't looked me in the eye since you came into the room."

She continued perusing the buffet, picking up a serving spoon to take some roasted vegetables.

He gently put his hand on her wrist. She looked straight into his blue eyes.

"Are we still on to take a walk after dinner? Please," he asked, caressing her wrist.

She hesitated for a moment before quietly saying, "Okay. I'll meet you outside. We don't need to make a thing of it in front of everyone."

He moved his hand away, and she took her plate and returned to the table. During dinner, she was much quieter than usual, and Finn noticed that she never once looked at him.

ELLA STAMPED OUT HER CIGARETTE butt and took the last sip of her drink. "I'm going to head up," she said.

"It's early. Stay, have another drink. It's Friday night," Michael urged.

"I'm tired. Oh, but I did want to ask about everyone's plans for the weekend. I saw on the call sheet that everyone's off for the next two days."

"Not me. I'm shooting a scene with some of the extras tomorrow," Albie said.

"Not me either. The director never gets a day off," Jean said.

"Yes, you do get all the headaches. The price of genius." Ella smirked at him. "What do the rest of you do on your days off?"

"I usually catch up on my yoga, meditation, and I run lines. Tomorrow I'll be reading your books," Charlotte replied.

"I haven't known what to do with myself," Willow said. "There's not much to do around here. I've never been on a location like this before. It's beautiful but kind of boring. Last weekend I just watched videos on my iPad."

"I'm up for anything. What do you have in mind?" Michael asked.

"There's a gorgeous private beach near the set. The weather's been so beautiful, and you've all been cooped up inside. I was thinking about asking the inn staff to prepare a picnic lunch, and then spending the day lounging in the sunshine. There's an old town about half an hour's drive from there that's supposed to be lovely, with shops, restaurants, and a cathedral. After the beach, we could change in your trailers and go have a look around, perhaps grab a bite to eat."

"Oh, that sounds fun," Willow said, beaming.

"I'm in," Michael said.

"Me too," Finn replied.

Ella looked up at him but quickly diverted her eyes to Charlotte. "Won't you join us? You have two days off. You can catch up on those other things on Sunday. It's so beautiful here. It'd be a shame not to experience it."

Charlotte thought for a moment. "All right. That sounds nice."

"Shall we all meet in the lobby at noon?" Ella asked.

Everyone nodded.

"Well, good night," she said, rising. She exited the room and discreetly slipped out the front door.

A few minutes later, Finn appeared. "Hey."

"Hey," she said.

"I'm sorry to keep you waiting. I didn't want to be too obvious."

"That's okay. You were right, the light is stunning this time of night just before the sun sets," she said, gazing up at the sky.

"Shall we?" he asked, gesturing toward the path to their right.

They walked quietly for a few minutes, their hands so close they were millimeters from touching. Finn finally broke the silence. "That was funny how you called Jean out for sleeping with his cleaning woman."

"I doubt it's much of a secret. Everyone knows what he's like."

"He has a bit of a reputation for how he treats women. You're such a strong person, and you two are friends. I was wondering what you thought as a woman."

"People want simple answers, but life is complex. He's created some of the greatest, most interesting, sensitive, and provocative roles for women in the history of cinema. There's a reason so many actresses are dying to work with him. And yet, he can be quite a piece of shit to women in his own life. Tell me, which is better: the male director who never casts women or does so only in clichéd, trivial ways but may be a hell of a good guy in private, or the man who creates professional opportunities for women that wouldn't otherwise exist and gives the collective imaginary new, powerful representations of women but uses up women in his personal life as if they were pieces of gum he was chewing until the flavor ran out?"

"Wow," Finn muttered. "I don't know how to respond."

"That's my point. When these are the choices, what's the answer? How do we define morality? Who's a good guy? Who's a bad guy? What matters, life or art? How are they related? What's public and what's private? Despite what many claim, it's rarely as simple as we might wish. Life is textured." She paused. "As for me, I adore Jean as a friend and as an artist, but you'd never catch me in bed with him."

Finn laughed. "I'm glad to hear that," he said as he gently let his hand graze hers.

She flinched and pulled away.

"Ella," he said, grabbing her hand. They both stopped in their tracks. "What's wrong?" She didn't respond, so he continued, "You've barely looked at me all night. Is it about the shoot today? I was horribly uncomfortable that you had to see that, but . . ."

"It's not that. I understand what acting is."

"I was thinking about you," he said. "Every time I kissed her, I looked at you and . . ."

"Finn, you have a girlfriend. Michael told me."

He looked down and sighed. Then he stared deep into her eyes and said, "I'm so sorry, Ella. I was going to tell you. I . . ."

She dropped his hand. "You don't owe me anything. Nothing happened between us. I thought there might be something, but I misinterpreted things."

"No, you didn't. Please, let me explain. Yes, I have a girlfriend. Her name is Savannah. We've been together for nearly two years, and she's been pressuring me to move in together and get married, but it hasn't felt right to me. I've known for a long time that we aren't right, but I've been too cowardly to end it. I tried to end things with her before I left, but she wanted me to wait until the shoot was over, which I agreed to do. I saw coming here as a break to clear my head and make a decision, but in my heart, I knew the decision was already made. I told Michael all of this. I'm sure he left that part out because he has the hots for you."

"His motives aren't the issue," she said.

"Ella, I was already thinking about ending things with Savannah before I came here. Hell, I even tried to do it. I swear to you that's the truth. Then I met you. I never expected anything like this, like the way I feel about you." He gently caressed the side of her face. "You're so beautiful."

"Finn . . ."

"I haven't even kissed you, and I'm already falling in love with you."

"Finn, please," she said softly. "Even if everything you're saying is true, I can't. You're with someone else, and that's a line I just don't cross."

"Ella, I don't love her."

"Then you need to figure out why you're with someone you don't love. But it can't be because, well . . ."

"I know you feel it too. The connection we share is not something that comes along every day. Maybe only once, if you're lucky."

Her eyes became misty. A tear slid down her face. He used his thumb to gently wipe it away.

"Come here," he said, and he wrapped his arms around her. She leaned into him and rested her head on his firm chest. He rubbed the back of her head. "God, it feels so good to hold you, like this is how it's meant to be." A few minutes passed before she pulled away. She gazed into his eyes, and he put his hand on her cheek.

"Finn, I don't want to be a part of something messy. And . . ."

"What?" he asked, tenderly caressing her face.

"If you could leave her for me, you could leave me for the next one. I don't want to set myself up to get hurt."

"I could never hurt you," he whispered.

She glanced down. "Please, let's be friends."

He sighed. "If that's really what you want, I'll respect your feelings. But please just spend some time with me. That's all I'm asking for. See how you feel."

She looked deep into his eyes, and after a moment passed, she said, "Okay."

"Can I hold your hand?"

She nodded and he took her hand, gently massaging her skin with his fingers as they continued walking.

An hour later, they were standing in front of the door to Ella's room. He lightly ran his fingertips along the sides of her face. "I've never wanted to kiss someone more," he whispered. "I can see it in your eyes. You feel it too."

"I wish I didn't feel anything. Finn, you're the most incredible man, and I thought maybe you were . . ."

"I'm what?" he asked softly.

"It doesn't matter. I can't. You're with someone else. I'm sorry." She went into her room, shutting the door behind her.

 **CHAPTER 8**

Ella trotted downstairs at noon in a white sundress and sandals, carrying a small tote bag and straw hat. The others were waiting for her.

"Hey, everyone," she said.

"Hey," they all replied. Finn caught her eye and remarked, "You look nice."

She smiled at him and told everyone, "The van is loaded. The kitchen prepared a picnic lunch, and they gave us beach chairs, towels, sunscreen, and a couple of umbrellas. Best part: I asked if they had something we could use to play music. They loaned us an old boom box. It's a relic. Wait until you see it."

"As in CDs?" Michael asked.

She shook her head. "As in cassettes."

Everyone laughed.

"It gets better," she continued. "They could only find two tapes, so I hope you all like Bon Jovi and Queen."

They all erupted into laughter.

"I think that's perfect!" Finn said.

"Yeah, me too," she replied.

"Let's hit it," Michael said, already halfway out the door.

They piled into the van, and Ella and Finn found themselves sitting next to each other. As they drove away from the inn, the van jostled over uneven ground. Ella bumped against Finn and put her hand on his thigh to steady herself. He smiled and put his hand over hers.

WHEN THEY ARRIVED AT THE PRIVATE beach, their driver set up the chairs and umbrellas. "The water is so clear. Look at those small islands in the distance. This is sublime," Charlotte observed. "I'm glad I didn't miss this. Great idea, Ella!" She smiled as they all started to shimmy out of their clothes, revealing their swimsuits. Finn sported blue swim trunks, Michael a black speedo, Charlotte a conservative black one-piece bathing suit, and Willow a turquoise string bikini. Michael and Finn couldn't stop staring when they saw Ella in a tiny white bikini, showing off her gorgeous, toned figure and flawless alabaster skin.

"God, she's incredible," Michael whispered to Finn.

Finn took a breath. "Come here for a minute." They stepped away and he quietly started, "Listen, Ella and I . . ."

"You two have something going on?" Michael asked with raised eyebrows.

"Not exactly, but she's special to me. Incredibly special. It's not just attraction, it's . . ."

"Say no more. I would never step on something like that for lust. She's all yours."

"Wow, thank you," Finn said with surprise.

"I should warn you that I may have inadvertently screwed things up for you. I told her you have a girlfriend. I'm sorry, I didn't know you had real feelings for her."

"Don't worry about it. I always intended to tell her. My relationship with Savannah isn't what I want, and now that I've met Ella, I'm certain. The way she makes me feel is how things are supposed to be, and I don't want to settle for anything less." He paused and sighed. "Honestly, I'm not sure if she even wants me."

"There's something between you two, the way you connect and get each other. Everyone has noticed. I didn't realize it was more than friendship and flirtation, but it's obvious she cares about you. I hope it happens for you guys."

"Yeah, me too."

Their attention was diverted when Ella screamed, "You know what they say about the last one in!" All three women sprinted toward the crystal-blue water.

"Holy shit! Look at them running," Michael said, his eyes popping out of his head.

Finn laughed. "You really do have a one-track mind."

"Come on," Ella hollered, waving them over, and they both darted to the water.

The women were splashing around. Finn ran right over to Ella, knee-deep in the gulf. He picked her up in his muscular arms and teased, "I think you need a good dunking."

"Oh, no, please don't," she begged, giggling hysterically.

He gently put her down and slipped his arms around her waist. They stared into each other's eyes and he asked, "Is this okay?"

She leaned onto his chest, warm from the sun, and curled against him. "No matter how I tried, I couldn't stop thinking about you last night," she whispered. They stood holding each other and smelling the briny sea air until Willow came over and splashed them, igniting a water fight between all five of them. They were laughing hysterically, the summer sun beating down on them all.

Mid-afternoon, Willow wanted to look for seashells and beach stones, and she asked Charlotte to join her. After they strolled off together, Michael winked at Finn and said,

"I could use a workout. I'm gonna go for a swim," as he headed toward the water.

"Alone at last," Finn said.

Ella smiled, got up from her beach chair, and unfurled a towel on the sand. She grabbed her book and looked at Finn. "Care to join me?"

He grinned and spread out a towel beside hers. He grabbed two more towels and folded them into makeshift pillows.

"Thank you," she said.

"My pleasure," he replied. They both lay down, side by side, facing one another. "What are you reading?" he asked.

"It's a poetry book, an anthology of the Romantics— Wordsworth, Keats, Baudelaire, Dickinson. They're my favorites. They tapped into so much emotion, imagination, and of course they loved nature. I think they deeply understood something about our relationship to the natural world and to each other. When I want to let go and get lost, I read poetry."

He smiled. "That's beautiful."

"Do you like poetry?"

"Very much. Early in my career when I was learning how to memorize lines, I used to practice by memorizing poems. I figured if I could master that, dialogue would be easy." She smiled and he continued, "Like you, I especially love the Romantics. May I read you something?"

She nodded and handed him the book. He flipped through it and said, "Ah, good. It's in here. When Albie was telling us about how he fell in love with Margaret, I started to think about how difficult it must be for him to be away from her and how much joy they'll feel to be reunited. This short poem by John Keats came to mind. It's called 'Sweet, Sweet Is the Greeting of Eyes.'

Sweet, sweet is the greeting of eyes,
And sweet is the voice in its greeting,
When adieus have grown old and goodbyes
Fade away where old Time is retreating.

Warm the nerve of a welcoming hand,
And earnest a kiss on the brow,
When we meet over sea and o'er land
Where furrows are new to the plough.

"Keats wrote that for George and Georgiana, his brother and sister-in-law, but it made me think of Albie and Margaret's grand love."

Ella smiled. "That was lovely."

"Here," he said, handing her the book. "Read me one you like."

They went back and forth reading poems aloud. Eventually, Finn put the book down and they stared into each other's eyes, a magnetic pull between them.

"Ella," he whispered, running his finger down her cheek. She started to lean forward when Willow came sprinting up, Charlotte following closely behind.

"Look, you guys! We found the most beautiful shells."

At the end of the afternoon, Michael said, "We need some tunes and entertainment." He put the Queen tape on at full volume and sang along to "We Will Rock You" as if he were performing at a cheesy karaoke bar. Everyone laughed. When "We Are the Champions" came on, he made everyone stand up and dramatically sing along. Willow, who only knew of Queen's music from the acclaimed biopic about Freddie Mercury, was pleasantly surprised to find she knew the lyrics. They were all impressed with her powerful singing voice. "Radio Ga Ga" came on next, and Ella squealed, "Ooh, I love this song!" She started dancing with abandon, and everyone leapt up to join her.

As the song ended, Finn whispered to her, "Would you like to go for a walk?" She nodded and they headed off along the water's edge.

"This was a great idea," Finn said. "Willow hasn't had this much fun since we arrived. Neither has Charlotte."

"What about you?" she asked.

He took her hand and said, "My whole world changed when I met you." They stopped walking and stood face to face. A breeze blew, and Finn gently brushed her hair away from her face. "I need you to know that I thought about what you said last night. The relationship I've been in, well, it's because I was afraid of ending up alone, but that's not half as scary as living without real love. I've made a decision. I'm ending it with Savannah for good. I would do it now, but after two years together, I owe it to her to do it in person. There's no time to fly back to LA, so it will have to wait until I get home. You have my word. It's over with her."

She looked down and he caressed her cheek, pulling her eyes back up to his. "You're not responsible. This was a long time coming. Ella, the way I feel about you, it's everything. Tell me you feel it too."

"I do," she whispered.

Unable to withstand the electricity between them, he cupped her face in his hands, leaned forward, and gently pressed his mouth to hers. "Oh my God," he mumbled, still holding her face, "I felt that in my entire body."

"Me too," she said softly, and they kissed again, more passionately this time.

He pulled back, and she traced the lines of his face with her fingers. They smiled at each other and he said, "If we do that again, I think we're going to need more privacy than we have here."

She took his hand and they strolled back to the others. Everyone smiled when they noticed them holding hands. "So, do you guys want to pack up and get ready to head to town?" Ella asked. "Willow, can I get ready in your trailer?"

"I LOVE MY NEW CLOTHES. They're so different from what you can get in LA," Willow said, happily swinging her shopping bag as they meandered down the charming cobblestone street.

"I hope my husband likes this print I bought for our flat," Charlotte said.

"It's lovely," Ella assured her.

"I always try to pick things up during my travels to support local artists and to remember the trips and the films or plays I made. It's like a tapestry of my life," Charlotte explained. "The stories I've helped to tell have become the story of my own life in so many ways."

Ella noticed some locals recognizing the four actors and excitedly whispering to each other, whipping out their phones to snap photos and take videos. She quietly said, "I keep forgetting you're all famous."

Everyone laughed and Michael said, "We'll try not to take it personally."

She shrugged.

Unbothered by the attention of her fans and fixated on shopping, Willow noticed an interesting store window and said, "Ooh, jewelry. Can we stop in this store?"

They all headed into the small shop; the walls were lined floor-to-ceiling with colorful stones, beads, and amber. The shopkeeper was speechless as the group of stars filled his tiny store. Willow pulled Charlotte to the corner to help her select beaded bracelets.

"Baltic amber is my favorite," Ella said, admiring a wall covered with brown, yellow, and green trinkets. "It's amazing what nature produces. Amber is so old, it's like wearing a small piece of natural history or a material reminder of the wonder of this miraculous planet. It has a calming effect, like we're all connected to something bigger. This one is gorgeous," she remarked, looking at a large chunk of green amber on a nearly invisible chain, behind a glass case reserved for the rarest items with the highest price tags.

"May I help you with something?" the shopkeeper asked.

"She'd like to try that on," Finn said, pointing to the necklace.

The shopkeeper unlocked the case and retrieved the piece. Ella lifted her hair, and he fastened the necklace around her delicate neck. She let her hair fall and turned to Finn. "What do you think?"

"It's stunning, like it's floating."

She smiled.

"I'm buying it for you," he said.

"Oh no, please, you don't have to do that," Ella replied.

"I want to," he insisted, touching her hand. "It's meant to be yours. It matches the incredible color of your eyes. And I don't want you to ever forget this day." He turned to the owner. "Please put that in a box. We'll take it."

"Thank you," she said, touching his hand. "I could never forget this day."

When they all spilled out of the shop, Michael said, "How about we grab some dinner?" They wandered into a bustling pub located in an old building with stone walls, cavernous hallways, and stone archways. The host nearly fell over when the stars walked in.

"We have a party in the corner paying their bill. We'll clean the table right away," he said. Several locals asked to take pictures with the group, which they were happy to oblige. Ella offered to play photographer. When they were seated, they ordered a round of drinks.

Two young blond women at the bar were openly staring at Michael, completely starstruck, tossing their hair and giggling in his direction. He smiled flirtatiously at them, and in a hushed voice, asked the group, "Would it be wrong to take those two lovely creatures into the bathroom for a few minutes?"

"Do you really just sleep with different women all the time?" Willow asked.

"The pretty ones," Michael joked.

Charlotte shook her head with a disapproving look.

"Oh, come on," Michael said. "It's a perk of being a successful actor. If they want it, why not give it to them? It's a release for me and probably a hell of a memory for them. I'm always honest about my intentions and safe about those things, if that's what you're worried about."

Ella picked up her drink, took a sip, and placed the glass down on the table with consideration. She looked Michael in the eyes. "There's more to you than you reveal, Michael Hennesey, perhaps more than you're even willing to admit to yourself."

"You probably have the most open views about sex of anyone at this table, hell, of anyone I know. If it's a consensual act between adults, what's the big deal? It's all about pleasure. Aren't you all for pleasure?" Michael said.

"I'm not judging you. Adults can do as they please, but I'm not convinced that it really is all about pleasure for you," she said. "You portray yourself as a man who doesn't care about anyone, who isn't attached to anyone and likes it that way. I don't buy it. Maybe it's not a woman, but there's someone who means something to you. The way you are with women, it's more than an overload of male sexual desire, more than casual rendezvous. It's like you're relentlessly trying to distract yourself. But from what, or more likely, from whom?"

He looked flabbergasted, as if she had read his innermost thoughts. He picked up his drink, took a big swig, cleared his throat, and said, "I have a daughter."

Everyone's eyes widened, surprise flashing across their faces.

"What's her name?" Ella asked.

"Sophie. She's eight years old." He paused. "I barely know her. I'm not a deadbeat or anything, I financially support her, but . . ."

"What?" Charlotte asked sympathetically.

"I was focused on my career when she was born. Things were taking off, you know? I wasn't really interested in parenting. And now . . ."

"Now?" Ella asked.

"Lauren, her mother, thinks I'm a dirtbag." He stopped to sigh. "Funny thing is, I had real feelings for Lauren. She's not like most of the women I meet now. She's sweet, the kind of person you marry." He paused, choosing his words carefully. "I was just too big of a shit. Women were hanging all over me, and I guess I thought, *I'm a big star. I deserve this.* I blew it with her, and now she doesn't want me to have anything to do with Sophie. When I'm busy with work, with women, I don't think about it. Other times it weighs on me, more so as the years go by and I realize that what's been done can't be undone." He polished off the rest of his drink and said, "It's too late to do anything about it now, so I try to put it out of my mind."

"Michael, it's never too late. You owe it to Sophie to do better. You owe it to yourself. The past can't be changed, but the future is unwritten. Make it right. You obviously want to," Ella said.

"She's right," Finn chimed in. "You need to man up, for your daughter's sake."

Willow huffed. Everyone looked at her and she said, "I'm sorry. I was just thinking about the film. Your character tries to cover up his pain with booze and bravado when dealing with my character and the state of our marriage, but really, it's an act. You should draw on how you feel about your daughter. It might push your performance further."

Delighted smiles swept across their faces.

"Was that stupid?" Willow asked shyly.

"Not at all. It was very insightful," Ella replied.

"You're really thinking like an actress," Charlotte added.

Willow smiled. "In the meantime, I have something you can give your daughter." She rifled through her smallest shopping bag and retrieved a small purple beaded bracelet. "I bought this for my friend's daughter, so it should fit Sophie. Here," she said, handing it to him. "You can give it to her as an icebreaker and tell her you thought about her when you were here."

"Oh, I couldn't," Michael said.

"Sure you can. Most girls her age like purple. Trust me."

"Thank you," Michael said, slipping it into his pocket.

The conversation moved on, and soon they were sharing lighthearted stories and enjoying Swedish bar food, including herring, prawns, meatballs, sausage, caramelized goat cheese, and an array of salads. Popular music played in the background all evening, and they just about died when Queen came on.

"What are the odds?" Finn joked.

"If you're going to be stuck listening to one thing, you could do a lot worse," Michael said.

"Agreed," Ella said. "Their music actually reminds me of Jean's approach to filmmaking."

"How so?" Charlotte asked with great interest.

"Well, Freddie Mercury was a brilliant performer, as were all the members of the band, just as you are all brilliant actors. But they were like a group of misfits who somehow created magic together. Looking at the five stars in this film, well, most wouldn't cast you as a group, yet Jean saw the potential for magic putting you together. What made Queen's music so special was that it was never one thing, could never be pinned down, because they always took unexpected risks. That's what Jean is trying to do with his body of work. It's why he works in the open, sometimes maddening way he does. He understands that an ordinary process won't yield extraordinary results. The only failure he sees is mediocrity, playing it safe. He's trying to get you to take risks, try new things, be willing to fall so you can soar."

They all sat for a moment, processing her words. Eventually, Charlotte sheepishly said, "That's why I'm here, why I took the role, but . . ."

"What?" Ella asked.

"Acting is my whole life. I have nothing else to show for myself. What if I discover I have no more to give? What if there's no more depth, no more layers?"

Ella reached across the table and placed her hand on Charlotte's hand. "Impossible. Like art, life is a process of discovery. There is always more. All you have to do is confront that fear." She squeezed Charlotte's hand and pulled back. "And you may feel acting is your whole life now, but perhaps you won't always feel that way. We can always remake our lives, if we choose to."

Every person at that table let Ella's words sink in, each deeply needing to believe them.

Finally, Charlotte smiled, raised her glass, and said, "Join me in a toast to this glorious day."

"Cheers!"

THEY ARRIVED BACK AT THE HOUSE and heard Jean and Albie in the dining room, laughing uproariously. "I think I'll go have a drink with them," Michael said. "Great day, guys."

Willow said, "I'm going up to my room to try on my new things and post on my Instagram." She hugged Ella tightly. "This was the best day. Thank you."

"I'm heading up as well. I'm going to call my husband before it gets too late. Ella, thank you for everything," Charlotte said, uncharacteristically letting down her guard and hugging her.

Finn and Ella lingered for a moment. "Everyone had such a great time today," he remarked.

"Yeah."

"Did you?"

"It was perfect," she replied, touching his wrist.

"May I walk you up?"

She took his hand and led him upstairs, unlocked the door to her room, and turned to face him.

He stroked her cheek and said, "You told Jean you should only sleep with people who you'll never love or who you'll always love. Ella, I'm completely in love with you. If you feel it too, be with me."

She pulled him into her room and shut the door. He brushed his fingers across her wrist, up her arm, and then across her cheek. He took her face in his hands, and they started kissing softly and with increasing passion, running their hands through each other's hair. He pulled his shirt off, and she slipped her sundress over her head. Gingerly, he unhooked her bra and let it fall to the floor. "My God, you're beautiful," he said, gently caressing the sides of her breasts. "I want to feel every part of you." He put his lips over her pale pink nipple, lightly licking it with the tip of his tongue. She moaned with his every touch. He picked her up and carried her to the bed, gently pulling off her underwear before hustling out of the rest of his clothes and lying beside her, staring adoringly into her eyes.

"Touch me," she whispered, taking his hand and putting it between her legs. As he moved his fingers in slow circles, she writhed and moaned with delight.

"That's it, baby. Let it out," he whispered, lightly kissing her neck.

"I need you," she whispered, pulling him on top of her. He slid inside her and moved slowly at first, kissing her softly. Their bodies found their rhythm, and he began to move faster until he could no longer take it and raised his head, screaming in ecstasy. They tried to catch their breath as he lay on top of her, both of their bodies quivering.

Eventually, he rolled beside her, and they lay quietly as he traced his fingers from her brow to her cheekbone.

"That was so special," Finn said, caressing her hair. "I've never felt anything like it."

"Me either."

"I love you so much, Ella," he said. "I always will. You're the one I've waited for my whole life."

She ran her fingers across his broad chest, leaned forward, and gently pressed her lips to his. Turning around, her back to his chest, she snuggled against his body. "Don't ever go," she whispered. He enveloped her in his arms, and they closed their eyes and fell asleep.

CHAPTER 9

Ella opened her eyes. She was still curled up against Finn, his arm slung over her body. She gently touched his hand to wake him. "Good morning, baby," he whispered, kissing the back of her head. She rolled to face him, pressing her body against his, their arms wrapped around each other.

"Good morning," she whispered.

"This feels so good. Did you sleep well?"

"Never better," she said, nuzzling closer.

"Me too," he agreed, kissing her forehead. "I could stay like this forever, with you in my arms. Being with you is the only thing I want. Nothing has ever felt more right."

She squeezed him. "I feel the same way." A few minutes passed and she said, "I'm going to run to the bathroom to brush my teeth."

"Promise you'll come right back."

"Promise," she assured him, slipping out of bed. She rifled around in one of her drawers and pulled out an oversized white T-shirt.

"Don't cover that beautiful work of art with clothing," he said.

She giggled. "Now you have something to take off when I get back." She blew him a kiss and darted into the bathroom. When she returned, she said, "There's an extra toothbrush in the top drawer."

He grazed her hand as he passed. "Thanks."

"You are the sexiest man I've ever seen," she observed, staring at his sculpted, naked body.

He smiled. "Hold that thought."

A few minutes later, he crawled back into bed. "Come here," he said, pulling her on top of him. He ran his hands down her arms and then pulled her T-shirt over her head. He swept her hair away from her neck and started nibbling on her earlobe. Her body trembled as he worked his way down her neck and then up to her mouth. They kissed passionately, running their fingers through each other's hair as they started making love. "Oh my God," Finn groaned as he held Ella's hips and thrust against her until they both let out sounds of bliss.

He enfolded her in his arms, panting as his breathing slowed. "I love you, Ella," he whispered.

She looked into his eyes and said, "I love you too. I love you so much."

They sealed their declarations of love with a soft kiss. "You've made me so happy. Tell me you're mine, baby," he said.

"I'm yours," she whispered. She sat beside him, and they propped themselves up against the stacked pillows. "Would you please pass me a cigarette?" she asked, gesturing to the pack on the nightstand. He gave her a cigarette and lit it, before lighting one for himself.

He glanced around and said with a chuckle, "Jean wasn't kidding. He really did give you the nicest room. It's way better than mine, and I'm one of the stars of the film."

She laughed. "Well, he's paying you. He had to incentivize me to come here."

"Let's stay here today, together, just the two of us. We can get room service sent up."

"I was thinking the same thing. That sounds like my idea of a perfect day."

They spent the day talking, eating room service, and making love twice more. As dinner time was approaching, Finn asked, "Do you think we should make ourselves presentable and join the others?"

"As long as you promise to come back here with me tonight."

He kissed her softly and said, "Sweetheart, you won't be able to get rid of me. Besides, you got the nicer room, so I'm planning on moving in."

She giggled. "Go grab some clothes from your room, then come shower with me."

"You have the best ideas," he said, kissing her again.

"Finn, do you think everyone knows about us?"

"Definitely."

"I guess it was pretty obvious when we were all out yesterday," she said.

"Yeah. I actually said something to Michael. I didn't want him to keep hitting on you."

"How chivalrous," she joked.

"Trust me, I was motivated by self-interest," he replied, running his finger down her arm. "And if they didn't figure it out yesterday, I'm sure everyone knows by now. We weren't exactly quiet, and this is an old house with thin walls."

"Oh my God," she said, burying her face in her hands. "I was so lost in the moment with you that I didn't think about anything else. I can't show my face at dinner!"

He laughed. "Don't be embarrassed. No one is going to think it was a hookup. They all know I'm in love with you."

"You think so?"

"Baby, Jean said something to me two days ago."

"What did he say?"

"He could see how I felt about you. He wanted me to know that it wasn't going to cause a problem with him if I pursued you."

"I told you that we're just friends," she said.

"I know, but guys can be weird about this kind of thing, and right now, he's my boss. He was just trying to make it clear that there wouldn't be any jealousy or anything like that, nothing that could affect our working relationship. Even though to you, you're just friends, he's as red-blooded a man as they come, and you are absolutely irresistible," he said, grabbing her and pulling her against him. "I'm sure he has come on to you before, even if you've made it clear you're not interested."

"Ages ago, sure. He jokes around, but that's just his way." She paused, and in a more serious voice, she said, "If you're concerned that this, us being together, is a problem for you with the film . . ."

"Don't even finish that sentence," he said, kissing her to stop her speaking. "It's not a problem." He looked deeply into her eyes. "Ella, I've waited my whole life for what we have. This feeling of oneness, just like you described in your book, is something I've never felt before. There's a profound sense of intimacy between us. We're lovers now, and that means everything to me. We belong together. Please don't get . . ." His voice trailed off.

"What?" she asked softly.

"Please don't get frightened away."

"Why would you say that?" she asked.

"Last night, when I told you I love you, you didn't say it back, even though I know you felt it. I could see it in your eyes."

"Finn . . ."

"It's okay, baby. I couldn't believe it when you said it this morning. I was prepared to tell you I love you over and over again until you were ready. It's not about that." He paused. "It's just that I get the sense you hold back your feelings sometimes, and it's also what Jean said to me."

"What did he say?"

"He said you're unattainable, that you'd never give yourself fully to a man."

"But I did give myself to you, completely. Couldn't you feel that?" she asked, a hint of sadness in her eyes.

"Yes, of course. That's why it was so beautiful when we made love for the first time and every time since. I don't want to lose you, that's all. I've only just found you. We've only known each other for a short time, and I realize there are many things about you I have yet to learn, but what Jean said resonated with something I already sensed. You mentioned that you've never fully given yourself to someone before." He paused and took her hand. "This is a lot for you, to give yourself to me—not just your body, but your whole heart."

"How can you possibly know me so well?" she asked.

"I just do," he replied. "Your heart is safe with me. That's what I'm trying to say, even if it's coming out all wrong."

She leaned forward and pressed her forehead to his, her hands holding his face. "I love you, Ella," he whispered.

"I love you too."

He kissed her lightly and said, "I'm going to grab some fresh clothes. Keep the shower hot."

WHEN FINN AND ELLA BOUNCED into the dining room, the whole group turned and started clapping, dopey smiles across their faces.

"Oh my God," Ella mumbled, looking down and shaking her head. "I'm mortified." Finn grabbed her hand and pulled her to the table, ignoring the laughter. They slid into the booth next to Jean.

Ella looked up, her face a deep crimson. "Charlotte, I would have expected more from you."

"Sorry," Charlotte said. "They made me go along with it."

"So, what have you two been up to?" Albie teased.

The group exploded with laughter.

"Working your way through the ideas in Ella's book, are you?" Jean asked.

Everyone laughed so hard, they nearly fell off their chairs. Finn looked down, blushing, but he couldn't help but laugh too.

"Okay, okay. You've all had your giggle. I'm begging you, can we please talk about something else?" Ella pleaded.

"We're just having a little fun," Willow said. "You guys are the cutest ever. I said you make a great-looking couple, like you were made for each other."

"And don't worry, we know the score: what happens on set, stays on set," Michael said.

Ella winced, but everyone was too preoccupied laughing to notice. Finn draped his arm around her, and the conversation moved on. Ella smiled along, but Michael's words hung heavy in the air.

AT THE END OF THE EVENING, as everyone meandered back to their rooms, Finn turned to Ella and said, "How about I see if I can wrangle another key to your room? I could grab some things from my room and meet you."

"Okay," she said softly. "I'll leave the door unlocked."

He kissed her forehead. "I'll be there soon."

A little while later, Finn walked into Ella's room and dropped his bag in the corner. Ella was standing at the far side of the room, gazing out the window. He came up behind her and slipped his hands around her waist. "Hey," he whispered. She reached her hand up and touched the side of his face. "Are you okay?" he asked.

She nodded silently.

"Ella," he said softly, turning her in his arms to face him. "What's this in your eyes? You look like you're a million miles away."

"It's just . . ."

"What, baby? Did they get to you? They were just teasing. I'm sure they didn't mean anything by it. You have a great sense of humor; you'd have done the same if it were any of them."

"Probably," she said with a half-hearted smile.

"Everyone's so happy for us. I bumped into Willow on my way up, and she said that they've all been secretly wondering when I'd have the courage to make a move."

"Is that what it is?" she asked. "Making a move?"

"That's not how I meant it, only that it was obvious to everyone there was a spark between us from the moment I laid eyes on you."

She looked down. He touched her chin and raised her gaze to meet his.

"Since we left our little bubble here, I think you've forgotten what it's like between us. Maybe you need a reminder." She smiled faintly, and he leaned forward and lightly pressed his lips to hers. They began kissing heatedly, tearing off each other's clothes. He knelt before her and put his mouth on her so gently that she squealed. She took his hand and led him to the bed, climbing onto it and lying down on her stomach. He moved her hair, ran his hands across her shoulders, and blew on her neck.

"I need you," she whispered.

He slid inside her and she moaned with pleasure. Finn pounded intensely until he screamed out in ecstasy, his body quaking. His weight pressed against her, he whispered, "I love you. God, I love you." He rolled onto his side and ran his finger down the length of her spine. They settled onto the pillows and crawled under the covers. Wrapping her in his embrace, he said, "I love you so much. Tell me you love me too."

"I love you," she said softly, burrowing into his chest. "Let's get some rest. Sweet dreams."

"Sweet dreams, baby."

 **CHAPTER 10**

The next day, Ella snuck onto set at four in the afternoon, wearing jean shorts, a tank top, and hiking boots, dirt on her face and grass in her hair. She stood on the sidelines, quietly observing. They were in the middle of shooting an intense argument between four of the characters. When Jean yelled, "Cut," she moseyed over to him. "Take five!" he hollered.

"*Ma chérie*, what on earth happened to you?"

She giggled. "I took a little trip to the forest. Research for my book about nature. I haven't had a chance to look in the mirror, but I can tell from your expression that I must be a mess."

"You wear it well," he said with a smile.

"How's it going today?"

He put his arm around her, leaned in close, and whispered, "What did you do to my actors?"

"What do you mean?" she asked nervously.

"They're entirely different performers today. The range, the confidence, the emotions they're tapping into. It's as if they've all finally let go, and they're accessing feelings far beneath the surface without doing any of that dreadful acting I detest. They're pushing themselves. It's been the best day of filming so far. I haven't reprimanded them at all." He stopped to laugh before adding, "I'm only sorry that Albie has the day off. He would have loved to see this."

Ella smiled.

Jean kissed her cheek and gave her shoulders a squeeze. "I know this was you—it has Ella Sinclair written all over it. Are you going to tell me your secret?"

"There's nothing to tell," she said. "Let me go steal a minute with Finn before you start filming again."

He kissed her on both cheeks. "After what you've done, whatever it was, take all the time you want."

She giggled and headed straight to Finn, saying hello to the other cast and crew along the way.

"Hi, my love," he said, kissing her and putting his hands on her hips.

"Hey."

He pulled a twig out of her hair, furrowed his brow, and asked, "What happened to you?"

"I went to the forest, looking for inspiration for my nature book. It's spectacular. Next time you have a day off, let's go for a hike."

"I would love that. I'm glad you're okay; I was getting worried when you didn't stop by earlier."

"Lost track of time," Ella explained. "Jean told me it's been a great day."

"Is that what you two were huddled together about?"

"Were you watching us?" she asked, running her finger down his cheek.

"Baby, I always watch you," he said, leaning forward and kissing her. "I can't take my eyes off you."

"You make that sound romantic, so I'm going to assume you're not a creepy stalker dressed up as a leading man."

He laughed.

"How's it been going on set today?" she asked. "Jean is over the moon."

"It's been awesome. Everyone's really plugged in now. Stay and watch the rest of the day."

"Given your expression when you saw me, I think I'm gonna head back to shower."

"You can use my trailer if you want," he offered.

"Thanks, but I need fresh clothes. See you at dinner?"

"Sure. See you later, sweetheart."

"Good luck with the rest of the shoot."

Ella arrived back at the house ready to head upstairs when she heard someone playing a melancholic tune on the piano. She peeked into the dining room and saw Albie sitting at the piano, a glass of amber liquor beside him. He took his hands off the keys when he saw her and slid over on the bench so she could sit beside him.

He looked at her and asked, "What the hell happened to you?"

"Adventure in the forest. How's your day off been?"

He shrugged, picked up his glass, and took a sip.

"Kind of early to be drinking, don't you think?"

"I'm on London time," he replied.

"It's an hour earlier there," she said, crinkling her nose.

"Ah, that's right," he said. His eyes were galaxies away.

She placed her hand on his. "Albie, please talk to me. What's going on?"

He sighed, picked up her hand, and placed her fingers on the piano keys. "Play with me, like that time in Barcelona."

Without another word spoken, she began playing the higher note keys on the right. She paused and he played the low keys on the left. They went back and forth, eventually playing simultaneously. They played in beautiful harmony, effortlessly in tune with each other. When the song ended, she took his hand and asked, "Are you ill again?"

"Yes," he replied softly.

"How long?" she asked.

"I started having symptoms about a week and a half before I came here. This is my third bout, so I recognized the signs immediately."

"Did you go to the doctor?"

He shook his head.

"Albie, why not? You should be at home getting treatment."

"That's not for me, not anymore. When I beat it the second time, I knew that was my last shot. I've squeezed all the time I can out of this tired old body. I can't go through chemo again. At my age, it's not how I choose to spend the time I have left."

"Then wouldn't you like to be at home with Margaret?"

"Working keeps me going. After forty years of marriage, she understands that. Rest assured, I'll spend my last moments with her, passing away peacefully in her arms." Ella smiled softly and he continued, "This will be my last film. I wanted to be a part of something special, just one more time, and create a piece of art to leave behind long after I'm gone. Jean knocking on my door again at this moment in my life was fate, I have no doubt about that." He shook his head and laughed. "Can you believe we're making a bloody film about the meaning of life and I'm dying? My character represents mortality, for Christ's sake. Bloody hell, it's true I suppose, eventually life does imitate art. Wicked, isn't it?"

"I'm glad you haven't lost your spirit." She patted his hand and chuckled.

"Never."

Ella gestured at the glass with eyebrows raised.

"It's not what you think, not really. I'm not drowning my sorrows or drinking day and night. It's pain management."

"Are you in a lot of discomfort?"

"This old bag of bones has seen better days, but I'm okay. I've been able to get through the shoots each day, sometimes feeling just fine. I need a little anesthetic in the evening to smooth over the rough edges."

"Oh, Albie. I don't know what to say. I'm terribly sorry." She leaned over and embraced him. He hugged her tightly in return.

When they parted, he smiled and said, "None of that, now. I'm an old man who's led an extraordinary life. I still am. And I must say, I was tickled when you arrived. I was hoping my last Jean Mercier film would be an Ella Sinclair experience."

"You don't want the others to know?"

He shook his head.

"I'm sure they would all be there for you, if you allowed them to be."

"Defeats the purpose. I'm here to make cinematic art with my colleagues and forget about this damn cancer stuff. Please keep this between us."

"Of course. I do think you should tell them at some point, but it's up to you. In the meantime, what can I do for you?"

"You're already doing it. Being around you is balm for my soul."

She smiled.

"Play with me again, Ella," he said, placing his hands over the keys.

"With pleasure," she replied.

EVERYONE STROLLED INTO THE DINING room to find Ella and Albie huddled together, laughing over a drink.

"Hi, baby," Finn said, sliding into the booth next to her.

She smiled and gave him a peck.

"I see you two started early," Jean said. "Tell us, what's so funny?"

"Just a laugh between old friends," Albie replied, lifting his glass and nodding at Ella.

"That's right," she agreed, raising her glass and winking at him.

Jean signaled to the waiter to bring their drinks. He turned to Albie. "Well, you missed a hell of a day on set. These four finally decided to stop acting and start feeling."

Albie chuckled. "How'd you manage that?"

"I'd love to take credit," Jean said.

"I'm sure you would," Ella interjected.

The actors laughed.

Jean smirked. "You know how these things go, Albie. Sometimes a fairy comes along and sprinkles a little magical dust that awakens the soul and reminds everyone what it means to truly be alive. But I wouldn't be so bold as to venture a guess as to what woke my actors up," he said, looking at Ella out of the corner of his eye. Finn slipped his arm around Ella, and she burrowed into him.

"Well, I will say this," Albie said. "Worse than missing the shoot today was missing out on Ella's beach outing. Sounded marvelous. I hope there are more on the calendar."

"Oh, I hope so too," Willow said. "It was so much fun."

"How about each time a few of us have a day off, we make an adventure out of it?" Michael suggested.

"I'd love to," Charlotte said.

Everyone turned to Ella expectantly, and she smiled. "Sure, that would be great. There are loads of things we can do. There are scenic boat tours, spectacular forests, quaint towns and villages."

The waiter served their drinks. They all raised their glasses and Albie said, "I'd like to do the honors. To living each moment, on film and in life."

"I'll drink to that," Jean said.

"Ditto!" they cheered.

FINN FOLLOWED ELLA TO HER ROOM. They kicked off their shoes, and she slipped her hands around his waist.

"That feels good," he said, kissing her softly.

"I, I . . ."

"What, baby?"

"I missed you today," she said. "I don't remember having ever said that to someone. Is it too much?"

He tucked a loose strand of her hair behind her ear. "It's perfect. I missed you too."

"Show me," she whispered.

They began kissing but were interrupted by Finn's cell phone vibrating in his pocket. He retrieved it, glanced at the screen, and turned it off.

"Where were we?" he asked.

Ella pulled away. "That was your girlfriend."

"Ella, *you're* my girlfriend."

"Finn . . ."

He sighed. "Yes, that was Savannah. Before leaving on this trip, I made it perfectly clear that we needed time apart and that I would be assessing things. The breakup won't be a surprise. The truth is that I already tried to end it, really, I did. She has a masterful way of tuning out what she doesn't want to hear."

"How can you treat someone you loved this way? It makes me wonder about you."

"Baby, I cared about her, but I never loved her, not by a long shot. I traveled so much for work that we have barely spent any time together in our two years. Honestly, I think she likes the spotlight more than she actually likes me. If you knew more about her, what she is like, I doubt this

117

would bother you so much. I'm not comfortable speaking badly about someone I've been with, so I don't want to go down that road." He paused thoughtfully. "And the truth is . . ."

"What?"

"I'm embarrassed. If you knew what she is like and how little she actually cares about me, you'd understand why I feel embarrassed that I've stayed with her for as long as I have. It reflects poorly on me."

"She's calling you. That tells me she cares."

He shook his head. "She wants to be on the arm of a wealthy movie star. It has nothing to do with me. I've only talked to her once the whole time I've been here, and that was before you arrived. She called me, not the other way around, but only to try to mend what can't be repaired. I want to be with someone I can't live without, someone who feels the same about me. This thing with Savannah was over before I met you. I promise that I'll unequivocally end it as soon as the film wraps."

"So, you're going to spend the next two months talking to her, texting her, lying to her?" Ella asked. "I don't understand how you can do that."

He took a deep breath. "You're right. When I decided to end it with her, my first thought was that it was only right to do it in person. Now I see that it isn't fair to you, and maybe even unfair to her." He paused and stroked the side of her face. "Ella, I'm in love with you. I'm madly, desperately, hopelessly in love with you. I know it's way too soon to say this, but I want to spend the rest of my life with you. In my heart, I'm certain we're meant for each other. We're soul mates."

"Finn," she whispered, looking down.

He took her hand. "Please don't be frightened off. I promise I won't rush you or pressure you. I just want you to know that all I want is for us to be together. This isn't casual or a summer fling. I'm all in. I'll FaceTime Savannah right now and end it. Then you won't be uncomfortable anymore, we won't have to think about this again, and she can start moving on."

"Wait," she said.

"I can call her from my room if you prefer," he offered.

"It's not about where you do it. It's . . ."

"What, baby?"

"Maybe your initial instinct was right, and you should tell her in person. At least don't do anything tonight."

"Are you sure? Sweetheart, I can handle this right now, and then we'll never have to think about it again."

She shook her head. "Wait until you get back to LA."

He wrapped his arms around her and said, "I don't know if I can wait that long. I want our love to be uncomplicated and free."

"Not tonight," she insisted. "Just don't do anything now. It's been a long day. I'm sorry I overreacted."

"You have nothing to apologize for. I know it's not an ideal situation, but when two people are meant for each other, they can't allow anything to stand in their way. Albie taught me that. Please, don't let this come between us. What we have is so beautiful. Let's nurture it. I love you, Ella."

She stared into his eyes and said, "Show me."

He slowly undressed her and took off his own clothes. "This is a once-in-a-lifetime love," he whispered, cupping her face in his hands. They began kissing, stumbled onto the bed, and made love tenderly, their eyes and souls connected. Finn whispered, "I love you," over and over again.

 **CHAPTER 11**

A few weeks later, Finn, Michael, and Willow had the day off. Michael suggested another trip to the town they had enjoyed. As they were wandering past the jewelry store, Michael said, "Do you mind if we stop in here? I'd like to get something for Sophie. Willow, I'll return the bracelet you gave me. It was very generous of you, but this is something I should pick out myself. If you guys don't mind, I could use your help."

"That's a great idea," Willow said cheerfully.

"We'd love to help," Ella said, and they casually entered the shop.

The clerk looked like he was going to pass out when the stars walked back into his store. "You're back!" he exclaimed. "Anything special you're looking for today?"

"I'd like to find a present for my daughter. She's eight," Michael said.

"Certainly," the clerk replied. "Over here," he said, ushering him to the corner. Michael spent half an hour perusing the selection and asking the others for advice before settling on a heart-shaped amethyst pendant.

He turned to his friends. "Maybe I should get something for Lauren too. What do you think?"

"That's a lovely idea," Ella said.

"I don't know what to get," he said, running his hand through his hair in exasperation. "I'm terrible at this."

"Well, what does she look like?" Willow asked.

"Wavy brown hair, brown eyes with flecks of gold, sort of like autumn leaves. Her complexion is similar to Charlotte's, fair with creamy skin. She's beautiful, in an unassuming way. She has delicate features, a long, graceful neck . . . oh, and she has the most wonderful smile, it's just slightly crooked. I used to joke that the only thing that could ever straighten me out was her crooked smile," he said with deep affection on his face.

Ella smiled. "Brown amber would suit her coloring. It's the big thing around here. Perhaps earrings to flatter her neck."

With everyone's help, he carefully selected a pair of dangling amber earrings and a matching bracelet. The shopkeeper gift wrapped the items impeccably in tissue paper and velvet jewelry bags, and the group spilled back onto the cobblestone street.

"Thanks, guys," he said.

"Our pleasure," Finn replied.

"I'm sure they'll love their gifts," Ella said.

"Where to next?" Finn asked.

"There was a little gelato shop up that way, on one of those side streets. Do you feel like something sweet?" Ella asked.

He ran his finger down her cheek. "Always."

"Ooh, I don't want to blow my diet," Willow said. "Do you mind if we separate and meet up in a bit? There are more shops I want to pop into."

"I'll go with you," Michael said.

Finn took Ella's hand and they ambled to the gelato shop. On the way, he said, "It was sweet how you and

Willow helped Michael. By the way he described Lauren, it sounds like he's totally hung up on her. It really surprised me to hear him speak about a woman that way, since he always acts like such a Lothario. It's a shame he screwed things up."

"People are imperfect. Truthfully, I feel bad for him. It must be agony to love someone that much and know that you've fouled things up. Something tells me he's going to make it right, or at least he'll try to. The jewelry is just a first step. Either way, I hope he becomes the father his daughter deserves."

They arrived at the ice cream parlor and marveled at the young man making homemade waffle cones in the store window, some dipped in chocolate, sprinkles, and nuts. "Those cones smell amazing. Mmm, everything looks good," Ella said, surveying the colorful offerings under the glass counter.

"What's your favorite flavor?" Finn asked.

"Mint chocolate chip. What's yours?"

"Chocolate all the way."

They each got a small cone and sat outside to eat. As they were enjoying their treat, Ella looked at Finn and said, "Do you think it's strange that we've been so intimate and have become so close, but we don't know little things, like each other's favorite kind of ice cream?"

"Sure we do. You like mint chocolate chip."

"You know what I mean," she said, glancing down. "There's still so much we don't know about each other."

"We'll learn," he assured her. "That will be part of the fun. All that other stuff is just details. Like when Albie was talking about falling in love with his wife. I know how we feel about each other. That's all that matters. It's everything."

"You don't know anything about where I live, what my daily life is like, what my family is like. And I don't know those things about you."

"Details," he replied with a dismissive wave of his hand.

"But what if . . ."

"What, baby?" he asked, reaching for her hand.

"What if you don't like some of those details?"

"Impossible. Anything that's a part of you, I will love."
She smiled.

"We have all the time in the world. The details will sort themselves out. But be warned, I'm sure I have all kinds of annoying habits. You'll just have to whip me into shape."

She giggled, letting go of the heaviness. They finished their treats in comfortable silence and continued meandering down rambling side streets. As they turned onto the main drag, a man stepped out from an art gallery, stopped in his tracks, and said, "Gabriella," his eyes wide with surprise.

"Oh my God," Ella muttered. She dropped Finn's hand, ran to the man, and threw her arms around him. She clasped him tightly, like she was never going to let go. When they eventually parted, she said, "I never got to thank you."

"There's no need," he replied. "I'm so sorry about what happened. It's good to see you looking well."

She smiled and stood for a moment, just staring at him. Remembering Finn, she said, "Oh, uh, this is my friend Finn." She paused. "I'm sorry, I just realized I never knew your name."

"Todd," he said.

"Finn, this is Todd."

"Nice to meet you," Finn said, extending his hand.

"Likewise. I'm a big fan," Todd replied.

"Thank you."

"Well, this is such a strange place to bump into you. What brings you here?" Ella asked.

"My partner's family is Swedish. We're here to visit them. I'd love to introduce you, but he's in there haggling over the price of a painting."

Ella smiled. "Well, it was nice to see you again."

"You too."

"Todd," she said. "Thank you so much."

He smiled. "Really nice to see you. I should get back in there and check on my better half."

When Todd stepped away, Finn said, "You hugged him with such sincerity, but you didn't know his name. Who is he?" She looked at him with a haunted expression in her eyes. He took her hand. "You're trembling. Sweetheart, what is it?"

"Would you mind if we went back to the inn? We could leave the van for the others and get a cab," she said.

"Of course. I'll text Michael."

When they got back to Ella's room, they both flicked their shoes off. Finn wrapped his arms around her and rubbed her back. After a long moment passed, she took his hand and they sat on the edge of the bed. "Do you want to tell me?" he asked.

She looked him straight in his eyes and began, "About four years ago, I was living in New York City. I was dating a man named Bill. He's a very affluent, well-known businessman, considerably older than me. He isn't the type of guy I usually go out with, but we met at an arts soiree and he pursued me relentlessly. We had only been going out for a few weeks. I hadn't even slept with him, and he was losing his patience."

He interlaced his fingers with hers.

"I decided he wasn't right for me, but I had promised to attend some black-tie charity benefit with him. I felt bad canceling, so we went. Afterward, he brought me back to his Park Avenue penthouse. He'd had too much to drink and started pressuring me again. I told him that it wasn't going to work out and that I didn't want to see him anymore." She paused as her eyes flooded.

Finn gently brushed away the tears and rubbed her back, patiently waiting for her to continue.

She sniffled. "He started screaming at me, telling me how lucky I was to be with him, how many women were after him, and that I should be grateful that he would even consider marrying me. He was completely belligerent." She stopped for a moment and shook her head. "I tried to leave the room, but he grabbed me by the shoulders and started shaking me, screeching that no one walks away from him. Before I could blink, he backhanded me across my face."

Finn winced and squeezed his eyes shut for a moment. Then he tenderly caressed the side of her head, tucking a strand of hair behind her ear before resting his hand on her cheek.

"He hit me so hard that I went flying to the ground. I just froze, couldn't move," she said, looking down.

"It's okay, baby," he said, squeezing her hand.

"He stood over me, unzipped his pants, and said, 'I will have you.'"

"Oh God," Finn mumbled, tears forming in his eyes.

"I started screaming at the top of my lungs. That man we saw today, Todd, came running in. He worked for Bill, maybe his assistant or butler or something. I'm not sure." She paused to take a breath. "Bill ordered him to leave, but I looked at him and whispered, 'Please help me.' He refused to leave and helped me up off the floor. Bill was ranting and raving, threatening to fire him, but Todd put his arm around me and walked me out of the building. He offered to take me to the hospital, but I just wanted to go home, so he hailed me a cab and waited until I drove off. I was so traumatized that I didn't even thank him or ask his name."

"Oh, sweetheart," he said, wrapping his arms around her. She held him tightly. "Thank God he was there. I'm so sorry," he whispered. "I'm so sorry."

Eventually, she pulled back. "I know I should just be grateful that I'm okay, that Todd interrupted him. It could have been much worse."

"What happened to you is horrible. I'm so sorry, baby."

"It really played into my fears, because . . ."

"What? You can tell me anything," he said lovingly.

"Trust in relationships has always been difficult for me, long before this incident."

"We all have things that are difficult for us. Do you know what makes it hard for you?"

She sighed. "I've always gotten a lot of attention from guys, since I was a teenager. So much of it has been unwanted."

"You're incredibly beautiful, so I can imagine how constant it has been for you."

"When I was in high school, there was this boy I liked, but I was shy about those things. He had been asking me out for a while, and eventually I said yes. We became a steady item. He wanted to be my first, but having sex with someone was a big deal to me. It still is. After going out for months, we slept together. I thought we were in love. Only later did I find out that he and his friends had a bet to see who could get me into bed. The whole school knew about it."

"That's awful," Finn said.

"I felt such a profound sense of betrayal. The worst part was, he kept trying to convince me that he loved me. He insisted he only took the bet because he wanted me anyway, and that by the time we slept together, he was in love with me. It was incredibly confusing. I felt so foolish, so naive. I wanted desperately to believe him, to somehow make it all better, but I couldn't even look him in the eye after that, so I broke up with him."

"He and his friends were fucking assholes."

She nodded. "Do you know the only thing that gave me any comfort?"

"What?"

"That I never told him I loved him, even though I thought I did at the time. I held it back, like maybe part of me knew better. I never gave him that piece of myself."

He caressed her cheek.

"It was such a formative experience because I was so young. Since then, I don't think I've ever fully trusted men or their motives. I didn't want to get attached, not to anyone. The truth is I've always been a free-spirited person, never locked down to a place or any one person, looking for amusement without responsibility. Wanderlust, I suppose. That's just my nature, always has been. In some ways, it's brought me a lot of joy and beauty."

"That part of your personality is infectious," he said.

"But there's another side. On some level, it's an excuse to not really give myself to anyone. There's a part of myself I protect, a piece I hold back that's locked away, deep inside. I'm always looking for an out, keeping my distance emotionally, ready to leave, waiting for the other shoe to drop. I don't give myself entirely to anyone. Especially since the incident with Bill, I've dated people, but I haven't allowed myself to feel the least bit close to anyone. I haven't wanted to." She paused. "Until you."

He kissed her forehead and rested his head on her shoulder. "Ella, I will never hurt you. I love you more than I can say."

"Finn, you're the first man I've ever truly loved. You're the only man I've said those words to. Ever."

"Oh, sweetheart," he said, kissing her lightly. "That means so much to me. Your heart is safe with me."

"Finn . . ."

"What, baby?"

"After the first night we spent together, you said you knew this was a lot for me, what you and I have. It is." She paused, then said, "I'm worried I'll disappoint you, that I won't be able to give you what you want, that the real me won't be the sparkling fantasy you imagined."

"All I want is to be with you. I know that's what you want too. There's nothing to worry about. Please, let's just be together always."

"Will you do something for me?" she asked.

"Anything," he replied.

"Lie down with me. I just want to feel close to you."

He turned the blanket down, took her hand, and they slipped under the covers. She nestled against his chest, and he enfolded his arms around her, holding her in his safe, strong embrace.

"I love you, Ella."

"I love you," she whispered in return.

THE NEXT MORNING, ELLA WOKE UP, yawned, and wiped the sleep from the corners of her eyes. She rolled over and discovered that the other side of the bed was empty. Confused, she sat up and peered over to the bathroom. The door was open, the light off. Empty. "Finn?" she called, her eyes darting around the room. He wasn't there. Her heart sank.

She dragged herself out of bed, shuffled to the bathroom, and brushed her teeth. Not sure what to do with herself, she curled up into a ball in the chair in the corner of the room, her head in her hands. A few minutes later, she heard the doorknob turn. She looked up as Finn stepped into the room.

"Hey, you're up," he said, smiling brightly.

"Yeah." She began to cry, unable to hold back the tears any longer.

"Oh, sweetheart, what's wrong?" he asked, rushing over and kneeling in front of her.

"I . . . I . . ." she whimpered.

"It's okay, baby," he said, caressing her face. "I'm here. What happened?"

"I thought you were gone," she mumbled.

"Gone?"

"When I woke up, you weren't here. You've been here every other morning. Last night was the first time we didn't make love before falling asleep, and I thought maybe . . ."

"Oh, sweetheart. How could you think that?"

She sniffled and looked at him through her tears. "I'm sorry. I . . ."

"This is hard for you. I know, baby. It's okay. Now I see just how much this is for you." He held her close, rubbing the back of her head. "I'm never leaving. I'm not perfect and I'm sure I'll make mistakes, but I'll never betray or abandon you," he whispered. "I should have left a note. I thought you'd still be asleep when I got back."

A moment passed, and she pulled back and said, "I thought maybe you didn't feel close to me anymore."

He smiled compassionately. "Sex isn't what makes us close. It's merely an expression of that closeness."

"I'm sorry."

"Don't be sorry."

"I can't imagine what you think of me. I've never acted like this before. I'm usually completely independent and carefree. I must seem needy and unhinged."

He chuckled. "Nonsense. Love can make people do all sorts of things. You'll learn to trust what we have."

She pressed her mouth to his and then took a calming breath.

"That's better," he said, wiping the tears from her cheeks.

She ran her fingers through his hair. "When I woke up

and you weren't here, I realized just how much I want you here with me. I love you. I really do. It's terrifying."

He kissed her again with increasing intensity to meet her passionate response. She rose and they undressed each other, tumbled to the bed, and made love intimately. After, as they cuddled under the blanket, Finn said, "Vulnerability is beautiful. It only makes me love you more. You don't have to hide your fears from me."

She took a breath. "It's so cozy here with you. This closeness is the best thing I've ever felt. I'm just worried about what it will feel like to lose it."

"Sweetheart, you're not going to lose anything. If you want to get rid of me, you're going to have to kick me to the curb, because I'm not going anywhere willingly." He kissed her and added, "You can't let your mind go to such a dark place. I can't promise I'll never be out of bed before you to take a run or something, but I do promise to always leave a note."

"Is that where you were? Running?"

He shook his head. "Hang on," he said as he leaned over and grabbed his jeans off the floor. He retrieved his cell phone from his pocket. "Come, sit with me," he urged, stacking pillows behind them. He slung his arm around her. "Yesterday when we were in town, you said you didn't know anything about where I live or what my life is normally like. A friend is house-sitting for me, so I called and had him email me some photos of my place. I live in Beverly Hills—I know how that sounds, but it's convenient when I'm filming in LA. I'm not into the Hollywood scene at all, just the work. See?" He scrolled through the photos, pausing to explain a few and describe his favorite parts of the house.

"Wow, it's gorgeous," she said.

"Thank you. It's about twelve thousand square feet, but I've tried to make it feel homey."

"You have a pool?" she remarked.

"Uh-huh. The outdoor space is my favorite. I have an outdoor kitchen with a few grills and a firepit, which is fun when friends come over. You'd love it. This is the garden," he noted, zipping through the photos. When they finished looking, he put the phone on the nightstand.

"It really is spectacular. It's so different from how I live."

"You said you're renting an apartment in Paris. Tell me about it."

"It's a loft, tiny, all one room. Only about six hundred square feet. The light is gorgeous, though. It has high ceilings with old wooden beams and huge windows. There's a small balcony where I have tea in the morning."

"It sounds charming," he said.

"I only ever cared about the location, really. It's in the eighteenth arrondissement, near Montmartre, and the whole area is just full of creative energy. You'd probably find it cramped now that I see what your house is like. I . . . I . . ."

"What?"

"Well, I don't have a lot of money, nothing like you or Jean. I just happen to have some wealthy friends who have splurged on me, like Jean, but that isn't my daily life. I've never really cared about that stuff. I own very few possessions, which works well since I move around so much. Living modestly has suited me just fine. My career has been successful and my work is well-known, but even still, writing philosophy books isn't exactly the path to great prosperity."

"I never expected it was. None of that matters to me. People should do what they love. It just so happens that successful actors are grossly overpaid."

"Finn . . ."

"I was hoping you'd come to Los Angeles and move in with me when the film wraps. Money isn't an issue. I'll take care of everything."

"Finn . . ."

"There's a large guest room suite that could be turned into an office: high ceilings, wood floors, big windows. It overlooks the garden and has a furnished veranda with a fireplace. It could be perfect for you. We could decorate it anyway you like. Or if you don't like that room, you could pick whichever you prefer."

"That's so sweet, truly."

"Don't worry, I know you were born to travel. LA is only a home base. I'm off on location shoots all the time, and you can travel with me. We can go anywhere else you want to, wherever you can find inspiration. Baby, I want us to live a long life of adventure together. I know how independent you are, but I want us to take care of each other. And please don't feel like you'd be giving up something without a commitment. I want to marry you. When you're ready, I'll propose."

"I don't know what to say."

"Have you ever been to California?" he asked.

"I was born in Laguna Beach."

"Really? Tell me about your upbringing."

"My mom's a painter, expressionism mostly, but with her own spin. There's a great art scene in Laguna, or there was at the time. She met my father at a gallery opening. She's very beautiful, and I guess he fell for her right away. He was married." She took a breath and continued, "Anyway, they had an affair. That's how I came to be. My mother says he always promised to leave his wife for her, but he never did. Maybe he just said what she wanted to hear."

He rubbed her arm and asked, "Do you know your father?"

"He came by sometimes when I was little. When I was four years old, he brought me a teddy bear with a white silk ribbon tied around its neck, the kind you might find in an airport gift shop. My mom sent me to my room, and I heard them having a horrible argument. Never saw him again. I guess he chose his real family. He'd had enough of my mother, and I guess of me too. I used to sleep with that silly teddy bear, like it would somehow bring him back. The ends of that white ribbon frayed because I held it so much."

"Oh, sweetheart," he said, pulling her a little closer.

"It wasn't that bad. I barely knew him. After that, we moved around a bunch. My mother was always trying to make something happen with her art. There was a restlessness to it all, like she was afraid to take root. But she had oodles of joy too; she was never one for the blues. She'd make each new place feel like home, painting murals on my bedroom walls in oranges, pinks, and purples, hanging twinkly lights over my bed, and building castles and forts out of whatever old things were lying around."

"That must be where you get your bohemian spirit."

"Yes. Mostly it's just what I've known. As a kid, I thought it was the best part of my mother, the free-spiritedness, the creativity. She's more settled now. She lives in Spain, in Valencia. It's beautiful there. She's been with a Spaniard, Alejandro, for many years now. I like him. She seems happy."

He caressed the side of her face and wiped away a lone tear. "It's no wonder."

"No wonder what?" she asked.

"That trust in relationships is hard for you, that giving yourself to a man is difficult for you. I don't want to play dime-store psychologist, but it's not difficult to see. Your father abandoned you. Then there was that asshole in high school. The other bad experiences, the many leering men. Put it all together and . . ."

"You think I'm damaged?"

"Cars can be damaged. Produce can be damaged. Even the bonds we create, like trust, can be damaged. People aren't damaged." He paused and took her hand. "People carry their past experiences with them, though, including their pain. It's part of what makes us human."

"So you don't think I'm messed up?"

"Of course not, sweetheart. You're exceptional. Falling in love with you has brought me nothing but unimaginable joy. But for you, there's another side. It's in your eyes and all over your face. You said yourself that feeling so close to me frightens you. With everything you've been through, it's perfectly understandable. I guess I don't know what I'm trying to say, just that I'll try to be sensitive to where you're coming from."

"Why are you so good to me?"

"Because I love you," he said, kissing her forehead. "This is new for you, and I know you're trying. Let me help. If something is too much, just tell me. If you're worried about something or uncertain of me, give me the chance to ease your mind without assuming the worst. When it comes to us, I only want you to feel joy, peace, and unbridled love."

She smiled. "That's what I feel right now."

"Me too," he said, kissing her lightly. "So, you're actually a California girl. What do you think of my place? Can you picture yourself there? Would you be comfortable moving to LA so we can be together?"

She squirmed a bit. "Finn . . ."

"It's too much?"

"I'm just not much of a planner. All I want is to be with you. Can we wait until the film wraps to figure things out? Right now, it doesn't make a difference as long as we're together."

"Of course. I'll get used to your spontaneous way of doing things. Just tell me you're mine. That's all I need."

"I'm yours, Finn Forrester." They shared a passionate kiss, pushing aside any remnants of fear or hesitation.

"It's beautiful out today. Maybe we could take a hike in the forest. Should we order up some breakfast first?"

She crawled onto his lap and said, "That sounds perfect. But first, kiss me again."

 **CHAPTER 12**

Later that week, when the group was finishing dinner, Albie said, "I do believe it's cocktail time."

"Tonight, something special is in order," Jean said. He hollered for the waiter. "Please bring the champagne."

"What are we celebrating?" Michael asked.

"The anniversary of the longest relationship I've ever had. Ten years of an exquisite friendship," Jean said, staring at Ella.

"Is it ten years tonight?" she asked.

He nodded. "I remember the date because it was the day before I received that ridiculous lifetime blah blah blah award. I asked the innkeeper to order a case of champagne to mark the occasion."

She smiled. "Sweet of you to remember."

"How did you meet?" Finn asked.

"It was in London," Ella said, lighting a cigarette and settling in. "You tell them."

"My friend Sandrine and I were supposed to have dinner at The Ivy with a small group of friends. She read in the newspaper that Gabriella Sinclair was doing a book reading at a local shop. Like all women at the time, or should I say all *interesting* women, Sandrine was captivated by Ella's first book of essays, which was unforgettably titled: *My Boyfriend or My Vibrator? Woman's New Existential Crisis.*"

Everyone burst into laughter.

Ella shrugged and took a drag of her cigarette. "What can I say? It was my first book, and I wanted to make a splash."

"That it did," Charlotte said. "I read it. It was riveting, I must say."

"Our little English rose. You are full of surprises," Michael said.

Charlotte blushed. "How on earth did you come up with that title?"

"I was dating some guy. I'll be diplomatic and just say we didn't have any chemistry, which he wasn't willing to acknowledge, so I ended it. He was feeling a bit wounded, male ego and all, and on his way out the door, he screamed, 'You better not write about me in your book!'" She stopped to giggle. "I guess we get something from every relationship. He wasn't a great lover, but in that moment, he inspired the title for my debut book. It became a best seller, and to this day, I imagine him walking past a bookstore and seeing it displayed in the window. I wonder what he thought when he saw the title."

Everyone laughed.

"Remind me to keep you satisfied," Finn whispered.

Ella nudged him and said, "Jean, tell them the rest of our story."

Jean continued, "So, Sandrine dragged me to the bookshop, which was standing room only. We arrived just as the store owner introduced Ella. She floated up to the podium in this long, flowy, backless white dress. I gasped at the sight of her. Not only was she the most beautiful woman I'd ever seen, but there was something hypnotic about her—the way she moved, her smile, the way she brushed her hair out of her face. Her eyes were dancing as if she were somehow more alive than the rest of us."

"Jean," Ella whispered, clearly embarrassed.

"It's true, *ma chérie*," he replied. He turned his attention back to the group. "When she spoke, I was utterly mesmerized, but I wasn't alone. She had the entire audience holding their stomachs from fits of laughter, all while revealing her laser-sharp mind. I simply had to meet her. Sandrine and I were stuck at the back of the room when a line quickly formed for the book signing, and I'm not a patient man."

"Ha! That's the understatement of the century," Ella interjected. "So, what does he do? He walks right to the front of the line, says, 'Pardon me,' to a woman waiting to get her book signed, and introduces himself to me."

Jean chuckled. "I said, 'I'm Jean Mercier, the filmmaker,' thinking she'd be flattered to see me in attendance, but she looked at me flatly and said, 'Congratulations.' My mouth must have been hanging open because after a long silence she said, 'Now that you've cut in front of everyone in line, are you even going to buy the book?'"

Everyone exploded with laughter.

"Needless to say, I bought the damn book. Bloody thing kept me up all night."

"Surprisingly, he also found the patience to hang around until I was done with the signing. He and Sandrine invited me to join them for dinner at The Ivy. Naturally, I said yes. Free meal, with an acclaimed filmmaker, no less."

Jean laughed. "We had such fun that night. We dined with a small group of successful artists, and Ella fit right in. Everyone was as enchanted by her as I was."

Ella blushed. "What I remember is the incredible food. I had been living on fish and chips wrapped in old newspaper, and you all know how extravagant Jean is. He ordered Oscietra caviar by the bucket, champagne and white truffle risotto, grilled lobster, filet of beef in béarnaise sauce, and on and on, not to mention bottle after bottle of champagne. He even toasted my book, which was very sweet."

"When the evening concluded, I offered her a lift home. I had the driver drop off Sandrine first so Ella and I could be alone. Then, on to Ella's. She was crashing at a friend's flat in the dodgy part of London. The next evening, I was being honored at a gala, and without my wife . . ."

"Second wife . . ." Ella added.

Jean laughed. "Yes, without my wife there, I was planning to go stag. I asked Ella to accompany me. Do you remember what you said?"

"I looked him straight in the eyes and said, 'I'm free, but I'm not going to sleep with you. I would like to be your friend. Perhaps we'll even be the best of friends if you don't fuck it up.'"

"I burst into laughter. I don't deny being attracted to her. I'm only a man, and Ella is a rare beauty. Truthfully, women rarely turn me down, so I was caught off guard. But I knew that having her in my life was better than not, so I agreed."

"That hardly stopped you from trying to feel me up the next night."

Albie shook his head in mock disappointment, and Michael spit his drink across the table, unable to contain his uproarious laughter.

"Well, a man can't be faulted for trying," Jean said.

"Hmm. I wonder if your wife would agree. Of course, you're divorced now, so we can hardly ask her," Ella mused.

They all laughed.

Jean turned to the others and said, "If you could have seen her that night, you'd understand. It was a formal, penguin-suit gala. The women were decked out in large ball gowns, the colors of precious gems. Ella, on the other hand, wore the most incredible vintage flapper dress, off-white with gold and silver sequins outlining her body. It fell just below her knees, with fringe at the hem that danced with every small movement. She wore an incredible gold head-piece around her forehead, and her lips were fire-engine red. When we walked into the ballroom, everyone turned to stare. She stole the room. Every man in the room fell in love with her in an instant."

Finn draped his arm around her and kissed her cheek.

Ella laughed. "When Jean invited me, I didn't know what I would possibly wear. I was twenty-four years old, had absolutely no money, and only one small suitcase that had jeans, T-shirts, and a couple of sundresses. I scoured the thrift stores that day and found that dress at a vintage shop for fifty pounds. It could have been a costume for all I know."

"You looked like fifty million pounds," Jean said. "I'll never forget it. Such style, such *joie de vivre*. When I heard you talking with people—royals, businessmen, artists, intellectuals, waitstaff—I thought I'd never known anyone better able to socialize with people from all walks of life."

She smiled. "After Jean received his award, I convinced him to ditch the uptight party and come hang out with my friends at one of our favorite cafés. They were in ripped jeans, and we showed up in formal wear. We sat for hours drinking cheap wine and talking about philosophy, art, religion."

"The *big* topics," Jean said.

"The big ones," Ella agreed with a smile. "They were playing popular music in the background, and when Elton John's 'Goodbye Yellow Brick Road' came on, I said, 'Jean, we must dance.' I mean, the lyrics were just too perfect, too ironic. Can't let a moment like that pass by."

Jean smiled. "We sashayed across this little café in our formal attire, with Ella singing every word. Can't imagine what the other patrons thought. It was quite the spectacle."

"Then there was the little awkward moment when he dropped me off and thought he'd cop a feel, but we laughed it off."

"Yes, well, like I said, a man can't be faulted for trying. I wasn't certain you had been serious about a platonic relationship. Indeed, you were."

"Indeed," Ella said with a giggle.

"But after we moved past my unwanted advance, I asked Ella to join me for my last evening in London. I had plans to go to the theater. A friend was directing a play, and I knew many of the actors as well. It was a terrific show, and after, the lot of us went to J.Sheekey. Such a fun spot when you're with a bunch of theater people. We spent the evening talking, laughing, and eating the most succulent Dover sole."

"It was great fun," Ella agreed. "Over dinner, Jean told me about a film he was shooting in Barcelona a few weeks later. I said, 'I love Spain,' and as if it were nothing, he said, 'Come along. I'll take care of the arrangements. Perhaps you'll be inspired for your next book.' What broke twenty-something in her right mind says no to that? So I went."

Albie smiled. "Lucky for me you did—that's the first time we met."

"That's right," she said, reaching over and placing her hand on his.

"We've been dear friends ever since," Jean said. "And perhaps there is something to Ella's sex rules. She's outlasted all the other women in my life, and I do believe we will always adore and inspire each other, despite the platonic nature of the relationship."

Ella smirked. "And they say you can't teach an old dog new tricks."

Jean chuckled, raised his champagne flute, and said, "To those who inspire us."

"Cheers, darling," Ella said.

ELLA WAS COZY IN BED reading a novel while Finn reviewed his script for the next day, preparing for a pivotal scene with Charlotte. After a while, she placed her book on her lap and sat quietly, absentmindedly running her fingers down his arm. "That feels nice," he said.

"I've gotten used to your nightly ritual. You always sip hot water with lemon as you review your script for the next day, making little notations in the margins. Chicken scratch, I can barely make out a word. Your eyes become intense when you're concentrating. I just love these sexy little fine lines," she said, reaching over and brushing the lines near his eyes with her thumb. "Then when you're thinking about something, you relax your eyes and rest the end of the pen on your mouth. This is my favorite part of you. This curve that dips down in the middle of your upper lip and this soft, raised spot right in the center," she explained, running her finger along his lip.

He smiled. "That's so sweet. See? We're already learning little details about each other's habits." He leaned over and kissed her. "Speaking of learning things about each other, that was a hell of a story about how you and Jean met. I can picture what you looked like that night, dancing in the café. I must admit that it wasn't easy to hear him swoon over you."

"Were you jealous?" she teased.

"Baby, I know you're irresistible, but that doesn't mean I want to picture other men trying to grope you. Even if it was a long time ago."

She giggled. "Speaking of jealousy, there's something I've been wanting to ask you, but I didn't quite know how. I don't want to sound ridiculous."

"What is it?"

"If you have any more intimate scenes with Charlotte, please tell me in advance and I'll skip coming to set. I know it's just acting and that it's your job, but . . ."

"We don't have any sex scenes. Honestly, we spend most of the film arguing with each other, like in tomorrow's big scene. Ours is not a happy marriage."

"I know, but if there is more kissing . . ."

He reached over and rested his hand on her cheek. "That would bother you, to see me kiss her? Even in a film?"

"Kissing, even touching her face . . ." She stopped and shook her head. "I know it's silly, but . . ."

"Shh . . . It's not silly at all," he said, beaming. "It's perfect, actually. Exactly how it should be between people who love each other, exactly how I knew it would be someday with the right woman."

"You're not upset?" she asked. "I feel so embarrassed for even bringing it up."

"Don't be. Honestly, you can't imagine how happy I am that you feel that way. It only makes me love you more."

"Really?" she said, touching his chest. "You don't have any on-screen love scenes, but how about we have one of our own right now?"

"YOU'RE ALL SET," MAJA SAID to Finn as she put the finishing touches on his makeup. "They should be calling you to set in about thirty minutes." He headed back to his trailer, where Ella was waiting for him.

"Hey, sweetheart," he said when he saw her sitting on the couch reading, her legs outstretched.

She looked up from her book. "Well, don't you look dapper."

"Thanks for coming with me this morning."

"My pleasure," she replied, scooching her legs up so he could sit beside her. "I know it's a big scene for you. I'm glad to lend moral support."

He wrapped his arms around her legs and rested his chin

on her knees. "There's something so incredibly nice about you hanging out in my trailer. I've never had that before."

"None of your girlfriends ever came to see you on set before?"

He shook his head. "I never brought any of them with me."

"That surprises me. Your work is such a big part of your life. You must spend most of your waking hours on film sets. You said you wanted me to travel to locations with you. Did you really mean that?"

"Yes, baby. I do, more than anything. I can't imagine being apart from you. It would be unbearable."

She smiled and stroked his cheek with the back of her hand.

"In the past, I've always kept my work life separate from my private life. I created boundaries to be professional, or so I told myself."

"What do you mean?"

"The truth is, I've never been with someone who I wanted to share everything with. Don't misunderstand: unlike you, I desperately wanted to find a life partner. It's probably why I've tried to make relationships work even when I've known they don't. But even though I've had longer relationships than you have, we're more similar than I realized. I've never really shared the fullness of my life with a woman. Wanting you by my side shows me just how different this is." He paused, staring at her with total adoration. "Having you here makes it feel . . ."

"What?" she asked, massaging his hand.

"Like everything in my life makes sense. It all fits together. Maybe it's like the wholeness you're exploring in your writing. Suddenly, everything in my life works together seamlessly, and I feel . . . serene."

She leaned forward and planted a soft kiss on his mouth.

"Now, speaking of the opposite of serenity, I should really prepare for today's shoot. I have quite the blowout with my movie wife."

"Let me help you run lines."

Finn smiled and handed her his script.

ELLA SAT IN JEAN'S DIRECTOR'S CHAIR, watching the actors find their marks. Jean yelled, "Rolling . . . Action!"

Having just stormed out of the party and into one of the nearby bedrooms, Finn was downing a whiskey when Charlotte cautiously touched his back. He flung her away. "Darling, please calm down," she pleaded.

"Leave me alone. Go back to the damn party."

"This is your family. I'm only here for you," she said.

"He's a smug old bastard. He's never appreciated anything I've done for this so-called family. None of them do. He'll hold on to the strings of his empire until he's below ground."

"Darling, I know the wounds run deep, but this is your family and it's a celebration. There's a ballroom full of guests. For appearances, we should probably . . ."

He turned to face her, contempt across his face. "Appearances?" he groaned with a loud huff. "Yes, I know all about your concern for appearances. Why else would you keep up this sham of a marriage if it weren't for *appearances*?" he seethed, guzzling the rest of his whiskey and slamming the glass down on the bureau.

She stepped back and softly said, "You've had too much to drink. You don't mean that. Pull yourself together so we can . . ."

"So we can what?" he raged. "So we can go back to pretending? You don't give a fuck about how things are, only how they look. Well, I'm done keeping up the charade." He dropped down in a chair in the corner of the room, hung his head, and ran his hands through his hair. After a long moment passed, he looked up and said, "How did I end up with someone so frigid? No wonder you're barren. What could ever live inside an icicle like you?"

Tears flooded her eyes and began spilling down her cheeks. In a faint voice, she whispered, "How can you say something so cruel?"

He inhaled deeply, rose, and put his hands on her shoulders. He softened his voice and said, "I'm sorry. That was awful. You're right. We should go back to the party."

She looked at him through a haze of tears, a lifetime of shattered dreams in her haunted eyes.

"Cut!" Jean hollered.

Charlotte wiped her eyes. An assistant handed her a tissue, and Maja darted over to touch up her face. When she was camera-ready, Jean yelled, "Good job. Let's do it again. Places. Rolling . . . Action!"

At the end of the fourth take, Charlotte crumpled over, sobbing uncontrollably. Finn put his hand on her back to comfort her, but she looked up, murmured, "I'm sorry," and ran out of the building. Everyone looked at each other in stunned silence, unsure of what to do.

Jean and Ella hurried over to Finn. "What the hell? Is she still in character?" Jean asked. "Damn method actors."

"That wasn't acting," Ella said.

"Maybe my performance was too much. I feel terrible," Finn said. "Someone should check on her. I can go."

Ella put her hand on his wrist. "It might be better if a woman went. Let me go."

Jean and Finn both nodded, and Ella set off to find Charlotte.

When Ella stepped outside, she saw Charlotte standing with her back to her, her face upturned toward the sun.

"I don't want to disturb you, but I wanted to see if you're all right."

Charlotte sniffled, wiped her face, and turned toward her. "Thank you. I needed some air. I'm so embarrassed."

"You have nothing to be embarrassed about."

"I've never broken character or run off set before. Never. It's just . . ."

"I'm a good listener, if you want to talk."

"I usually keep things pretty close to the vest. We English aren't like you Americans. Stiff upper lip and all."

Ella smiled kindly.

"The scene hit pretty close to home," Charlotte continued. "My husband is a playwright and director. We've always been married to our work. In the beginning, that's how we both wanted it."

"And now?" Ella asked.

"Perhaps there's more to life. Perhaps I'm missing out on something. I've been thinking that I'd like to have a child. When I broached it with him, he immediately countered with all the ways it would interfere with my career. I looked into adoption as a possibility, but I'm not really sure if that's the answer. Maybe he doesn't want a child, or maybe he just doesn't want one with me. I honestly don't know. I'm terrified to find out."

Ella embraced her in a warm hug. Charlotte wrapped her arms around her in return. The women held each other in the summer sunshine, breathing the fresh, free air. When they parted, Ella said, "A child isn't something you should give up on. Try to use the time you have here to build up the courage to confront this when you go home."

"I'm not even sure if I'd be a good mother." Charlotte paused and shook her head. "Have you ever felt that way, like there's something you desperately want but you don't know if you're up to it?"

"Yes," Ella said softly. "Finn is planning a whole life for us, and I want it so badly. I love him, but . . ."

"You're not sure you can do it? Like you don't know how to have that life and still be who you are. You can't trust that you're totally ready for it, or that he'll be able to pick up the slack if you falter. Right?"

Ella nodded.

"Well, I know I must seem like the last person to give advice right now, but I'm certain that Finn loves you. Pretty clear that you love him too."

Ella smiled. "If the scene is too much for you, I can talk to Jean. Maybe he already got what he needs."

"Thank you, but the one thing I can do is act, and that's exactly what I need to do now. I'm just worried about what they'll all think with the way I behaved."

"Don't give it another thought. They're human. They'll understand. If you were an American actress, you wouldn't think twice about it. Everyone would just assume that you're temperamental and move on."

Charlotte laughed. "Ella, will you keep this between us? I wouldn't want . . ."

"Of course. Shall we head back in?"

Charlotte nodded and they walked back inside. Everyone turned to look.

Finn rushed over. "Are you all right? I'm sorry if . . ."

"She's fine. She just needed a moment," Ella said.

Charlotte turned to Jean and said, "I apologize. After a makeup retouch, I'm ready to get back to work."

"Places, everyone," Jean called.

FINN DROPPED HIS SCRIPT ON THE nightstand and slung his arm around Ella. She put her book down and gazed into his eyes.

"Are you sure Charlotte's okay?" he asked. "She killed it today when she got back to set, but she was pretty quiet at dinner."

"She's just working some personal things out. She'll be all right. I would tell you, but I promised her . . ."

"It's okay, baby," he said, kissing her softly. "It was sweet of you to help her. I really felt terrible."

"You didn't do anything wrong. Sometimes art strikes a nerve or pulls the scab off a wound that's not yet healed, that's all."

"It can get pretty intense on location like this. I've seen actors affected in all sorts of ways."

She looked down as if searching for the words. "Yeah, this place isn't exactly real life. You're all immersed in this powerful story you're telling, living in this surreal environment, away from your loved ones, away from your true selves. I can understand how emotions become heightened. Finn, if that's what's happening with us . . ."

"Oh, no, baby, not in the least. Don't think that for a second. So much of my life has happened on locations, and trust me, this is very much my real life. More than anything, *you* are my real life."

She smiled faintly.

"What are you thinking?" he asked.

She looked deep into his eyes and said, "Finn, why do we love each other?"

"Because we can't help it. We can't help it but to love each other." He kissed her softly and then rested his forehead against hers. He lingered for a long, intimate moment, and whispered, "Because we do. We just do."

"Yes, but . . ."

"Does it really matter? We feel what we feel."

"I know, but . . ."

"Do you really need to know why?" he asked. "I don't know if I could explain it."

"I've spent my entire adult life asking big questions about human existence, searching for reason, and now . . ." She sighed and thought for a moment, the words escaping her again. "My life was one thing and now it's something else, and your life was also one thing and now it's something else, just because we met, because of this inexplicable feeling we have for each other. How does that happen?"

"I don't know. The only thing I know for sure is that what we have together is bigger than what I have without you. How we feel about each other, it's everything, Ella."

"You've been with so many women. Why me and not any of them?"

"Because I'm in love with you," Finn said. "The best way I can explain it is to say that when we're together, it's like I have the answer to a question I didn't know I was asking."

She smiled. "That's so romantic. But . . ."

"What, baby?"

"The first night we were together, you said you love me and you always will. How can you possibly know that?"

"I trust what we have."

She looked down.

He touched her chin and raised her gaze to meet his. He ran his finger across her lips and kissed her lightly. "That, right there, Ella. That feeling when our lips touch, that feeling I have in my entire body. I can see it in your eyes, you feel it too. I don't need to know anything else. Do you?"

"No," she whispered, and she pressed her mouth gently to his.

"Come on, sweetheart, let's get some sleep. We can cuddle." He reached over to turn off the lights and then lay down behind her, holding her close and feeling her heart beat.

 **CHAPTER 13**

All five actors finally had a day off together while Jean filmed exterior shots with the extras. Ella planned an outing and told everyone to dress casually with comfortable walking shoes. The first stop was a nearby forest for a light morning hike along a nature trail.

"You go ahead with the others," Ella whispered to Finn. "I'm going to take my time with Albie."

While the others walked ahead, Ella and Albie casually strolled behind the group, their arms locked.

"You're a dear to walk with me," Albie said.

"I'm glad to have this time with you," she replied.

Albie looked up, the trees so tall he could hardly see where they ended and the sky began. He took a deep breath and said, "Being out in nature always reminds me of the seasonality of our lives, how we must learn to let go again and again so we may ready ourselves for what comes next." She smiled and patted his arm. He continued, "This must be good inspiration for your book about the pleasure to be found in nature. Have you had any great insights?"

"I don't know if it qualifies as a great insight, but I think there's something powerful about feeling how small we are that helps us let go of ourselves and become part of something much larger. It somehow makes us feel less important and yet more alive, all at once."

Albie huffed. "One could say the same thing about love."

"You think so?"

"I most certainly do. We all carry so much shit with us—our egos, our fears, our shame—all that nonsense. When you fall in love, it suddenly isn't all about you anymore and that's such a relief. You're forced to let go, to realize you're part of something bigger. You come to understand that what you share, and indeed that other person, is more important than you are."

"But if the other person becomes your world, do you lose yourself?" she asked.

"If the relationship is right, you become their world too. It's about partnership. That safe, secure bond allows you to become more of yourself, not less."

"Is that what it was like when you fell in love with Margaret?"

"I made some mistakes in the beginning, no doubt. It took me a little while to adjust. Being a pampered actor and all, I was used to things revolving around me."

She laughed.

"Margaret is patient. She taught me how to put another person first. Like all good teachers, she led by example."

"She's a wonderful woman. I was glad to have met her that time in the Cotswolds."

"She always speaks fondly of you. She would love it here. When we were younger, we used to vacation in the countryside. She used to make these wonderful picnics for us; every item was homemade and carefully wrapped. She'd even fold our paper napkins just so. She's so good at the little things, the things that make everything special. We'd sit outside for hours, just being together."

Ella smiled.

Albie leaned closer and said, "Finn is quite a guy."

"Yes, he is," she replied, squeezing his arm.

Albie patted her hand. "Jean thinks the biggest question is: What is the meaning of life? The truth is, that's an easy one to answer. Human beings want to feel connection—to our work, to our world, and mostly, to each other. Simple, really. Perhaps there's an even bigger question."

"What's that?" she asked.

He chuckled. "Spoils the fun if you get all the answers from an old fucker like me."

She laughed.

"So, what's next on the agenda?" he asked.

"A scenic boat tour to a small residential island where I've booked lunch at a historic hotel with spectacular water views."

"THAT CRUISE WAS LOVELY," CHARLOTTE remarked as they were seated for lunch.

"It's been such a wonderful day. I didn't realize how calming nature can be," Willow said.

"Did you notice those huge estates along the water's edge?" Albie asked. "My Margaret would have loved all those gardens. She's been blessed with a green thumb, just one of her many talents."

"You must miss her terribly," Ella remarked.

"Every minute. We talk every night, but I can be quite a pain in the ass. It's a wonder she's put up with me all these years. She's probably glad to be rid of me for a while and have some peace and quiet."

"Doubtful," Ella said.

The host came by and handed them each a menu. "Would you please take a picture of us?" Willow asked, handing him her phone.

"Certainly."

"Take a few, please. Come on, guys. Everyone smile! I want a memento to remember this summer by."

Finn draped his arm around Ella, and the rest crowded around them. When the host returned her phone, she scrolled through the shots and said, "Ooh, they're good. I'll send you all the best one. Mind if I post this on my social?"

"Sure," Michael replied.

"Go ahead," Finn said.

The others nodded their agreement.

As the group focused on their menus, Finn leaned over and whispered to Ella, "What are you thinking of ordering?"

"Their marinated salmon is just divine. I'll miss it when we leave Sweden. You?"

"Shrimp sandwich."

"That sounds good."

"I think I'm going to have the Swedish meatballs with lingonberries and mashed potatoes," Albie said. "Margaret disapproves of how I eat when I'm left to my own devices, but that sounds too good to pass up."

"Lauren, my ex, used to do that. She'd always tell me I can't live on cheeseburgers, but in a sweet way, like she was looking out for me," Michael said.

The women all smiled at him.

Albie tapped on the table. "I know it's a funny thing for an actor to say, but love isn't always how the movies make it seem. The feelings, yes, but the day-to-day *doing* of love shows itself in other ways. Sometimes love is someone saying, 'You shouldn't eat so much salt,' or, 'Don't drink too much, you've had enough.' Every time Margaret prepares a meal for me, it's an act of love. Of course, she's my savior, I can hardly boil eggs."

Everyone laughed.

"It must be a weird actor thing—we're so focused on being someone other than ourselves that we never learn the basic skills of human survival," Finn joked. "Thank God I have a private chef, or I'd be lost."

"You have a private chef?" Ella asked, sounding surprised.

"Yeah. I have a small staff."

"Oh," Ella said, looking down.

"You'll meet them," he said, rubbing her arm. "Do you like to cook?"

"Love to."

"Ella throws the most marvelous dinner parties, complete with themes and takeaway gifts," Albie said.

"That sounds like fun. Tell us about them," Willow said.

"I love entertaining. Sometimes I make all the food myself, and other times I ask everyone to bring something. I don't do potlucks as much anymore after one disastrous get-together. I was throwing a cheese and wine party, and I asked everyone to bring either a cheese or a type of charcuterie. To my dismay, everyone showed up with Brie. We had wine, crackers, and about ten wheels of Brie!"

Everyone laughed.

"I've done all kinds of themes: roaring twenties, midnight in Morocco, literary costume party, children's lit book club. I decorate to go with the theme, usually finding inexpensive trinkets at party supply stores, flea markets, or antique shops. It makes it festive and gives people something to talk about, kind of like an icebreaker. I always make little party favors for my guests to take home with them, even if it's just something small like a chocolate truffle or a copy of a poem."

"That's so nice," Finn said, putting his arm around her.

"When you showed me photos of your house, I thought it would be an amazing location for a Great Gatsby party. Everyone could dress up, and we could serve finger foods and buckets of champagne."

He smiled brightly. "Count me in. I'm an actor, so you know I love playing dress-up. You'd be an amazing Daisy."

"I've never thrown a party in a house like yours. It would be such fun." She turned back to the group. "No matter how small my apartment is, I find a way to cram a big group in. I once cooked a seven-course tasting menu on my one little burner in my Parisian loft. That was a challenge. Sometimes it's simpler, and I'll just make a cake and have people over for coffee and tea. When you get a group of artists and intellectuals together, it doesn't take much—you can spend hours talking, just nibbling on a baguette."

"Or ten wheels of Brie!" Michael joked.

They all laughed.

"This is a damn fun group," Albie said. "I so enjoy breaking bread with all of you."

Everyone smiled and nodded their agreement, and Willow asked, "Do you think we'll all ever be together again?"

"What do you mean?" Charlotte asked.

"Well, I haven't done as many films as you guys have, so I'm not sure what it's usually like. We've all become such good friends. It's hard to imagine not seeing you all every day. The film wraps in a couple of weeks, and I was just wondering if we'll still be in each other's lives."

Finn sighed. "The truth is, you often get close to people on a film set. Sometimes you stay in touch, but usually you're on to the next project and, well . . ."

Willow looked down.

"But this is different," Finn added. "I've never had an experience like this before. I think we'll stay in each other's lives. The film centers on a big celebration, and something tells me we'll all be together one day for a real one."

Ella looked at him and smiled.

"Absolutely," Michael said. "We'll stay friends. We'll make a point of it."

"Indeed," Charlotte agreed.

Willow smiled. They spent the next few hours eating and talking about everything from travel to art to philosophy. When the restaurant finally closed, the group strolled around the island for a bit before catching the boat back. Finn and Ella found a cozy spot near the front of the boat where they could be alone.

"Did you mean what you said to Willow, that we'll all stay in each other's lives?" Ella asked.

"Sweetheart, you're stuck with me. But yes, I think we'll stay friends with the others. I predict that one day, not so long from now, we'll all reunite at a huge bash and dance the night away just like we did back at the inn for Albie's birthday."

"I hope so," she said.

"I loved hearing about the parties you've thrown. I like entertaining too, though I usually keep it to barbecues out back. There's that great firepit I told you about too. It's a fun place to sit around, drink, talk, and toast marshmallows. My friends are cool. I think you'll like them."

She smiled.

"You seemed less than enthusiastic when I mentioned my chef."

"It's just . . ."

"What, baby?"

"Well, you have a whole life that's all set up, obviously the way you like it. It's nothing like what I'm used to, nothing like my life. I'm just not sure how I would fit into that."

He squeezed her tightly and kissed her forehead. "Sweetheart, when we live together, it won't be my house, it will be ours. And if it's a problem, we can buy a new house together, one that's just ours."

"But . . ."

"As for the staff, we can make any arrangement you want. You can do however much cooking you want to do.

Hell, you might like having a sous-chef. We'll figure it out. I'm not married to anything the way it is. That was my life alone; this would be our life together. Naturally, some things will have to change. Please don't think you'd have to fit into my old life. That's not what I want. I want us to build a new one together."

"You do?" she asked, gazing into his eyes.

"Of course I do," he replied, kissing the top of her head. "All that matters is that we're together. We can figure out what works best for us. That's part of the adventure."

 CHAPTER 14

The next morning, Ella and Finn were hanging out in his trailer when he was called to set. As they were walking toward the estate, the door to the makeup trailer flew open and two small children burst out and ran across the grassy field, their blonde ringlets blowing in the breeze. Maja raced after them, hollering in a mix of Swedish and English. Ella and Finn sprinted over to help just as Maja caught up with the kids.

"Who are these little ones?" Ella asked sweetly.

"These are my kids. Astrid is four and a half, and Lars is nearly two. My babysitter had an emergency and sprang them on me fifteen minutes ago. I've tried calling everyone I know, but I haven't found anyone who can take them. I don't know what to do. I'm expected to be on set all day for touch-ups. If Mr. Mercier finds out, I'm sure I'll lose my job."

"I'll watch them," Ella said. "And don't worry about Jean. I can handle him."

"Oh no, I couldn't impose on you. I'll figure something out."

"Don't be silly," Ella insisted, plopping onto the grass. She picked a small dandelion from the ground and handed it to Lars. When she blew on it and the fuzzy white poofs dispersed into the air, he laughed hysterically and fell into her arms. "Again!" he squealed. She picked another dandelion and handed it to him.

Astrid sat beside Ella and said, "You look like a princess."

"Well, so do you," Ella replied.

Astrid giggled.

Ella looked up at Maja. "See? We're already friends."

Finn smiled widely, taking in the joyful scene.

"Well, maybe you could just watch them for a bit while I keep calling people," Maja said.

"There's no need. I love children. We'll have a splendid day together," Ella assured her. She laughed at Lars, who was spitting on his dandelion, trying to make the poofs fly into the air. When he finally gave up, she said, "Finn, can we hang out in your trailer?"

"Of course."

"My babysitter dropped them off with a bag—toys, books, a change of clothes, their lunch, and some snacks," Maja said.

"Why don't I grab their things while you get them settled in my trailer?" Finn suggested.

"I don't know what to say. Thank you both so much," Maja gushed.

"It's my pleasure," Ella replied as she handed both children new dandelions to blow. "We can hang out in Finn's trailer, play out in the field, maybe pick some berries. We'll have a great day."

A few minutes later, Ella, the kids, and their bag were settled in Finn's trailer. Lars immediately pulled a book out of the bag and pushed it toward Ella. She sat down on the couch, a child on either side of her, and began to read. Finn leaned down to kiss her forehead, and then he and Maja headed off to the set. Before closing the door, he turned around to take one last look at Ella and the kids, adoration and an irrepressible smile on his face.

At two o'clock, Finn returned to the trailer with lunch. When he walked in, Ella was sitting on the couch, her legs outstretched. Astrid was lying beside her, and Lars was curled up on top of her sucking his thumb, both sound asleep.

"Shh . . ." she whispered, holding her finger to her mouth.

He kissed her forehead again and knelt on the floor beside them. "This is the sweetest sight," he whispered.

"We played outside for ages, and they passed out after I gave them lunch."

"Maja will be here in a few minutes. She got in touch with her sister, and she's coming to get them."

"All right. Let's let them rest until they have to go," she said, stroking Lars's hair.

Soon Maja arrived to collect the children, who were reluctant to leave and smothered Ella with hugs. "Thank you again. You really saved me," Maja said on her way out.

Finn cozied up beside Ella on the couch. He wrapped his arms around her and kissed her softly. "Those kids are crazy about you."

"They're adorable. We had fun together," she said, yawning. "They did wear me out, though. I could use a nap myself. I might head back to the inn after lunch."

"What do you say we skip the group dinner tonight and do something just the two of us? I can make our excuses with Jean."

"Okay," she said, barely able to contain another yawn. "What do you have in mind?"

"A candlelit dinner in your room, maybe a bubble bath in that big clawfoot tub."

"That sounds romantic."

"I'll take care of everything."

LATER THAT NIGHT, ELLA WAS relaxing in her room when there was a knock on the door. She opened it to find a waiter with a tray. "Mr. Forrester asked me to deliver this. He hired a local chef to prepare a special meal for you two."

"Oh, wow," Ella said. "Please come in. You can put it right over there on the table."

He set the table for their dinner, thoughtfully arranging two plates under silver cloches, an ice bucket with a bottle of champagne, two flutes, and a small vase with brightly colored wildflowers. Then he removed two candlesticks from his pockets, which he placed in holders on the table. He lit the candles and asked, "Is there anything else I can get you, Miss Sinclair?"

"No, thank you so much."

He turned on his heel and left, closing the door silently behind him.

Ella picked up the vase to smell the flowers but paused when she heard the door open. Finn walked in with an armful of votive candles. "Hi there. I can't believe you did all this."

"Hi, sweetheart," he said, kissing her softly. "It was nothing."

"The flowers are so beautiful."

"I'm glad you like them," he said. "I figured if we had met somewhere else, I would have asked you out on a proper date and I would have brought you flowers."

"That's so sweet. What are all those for?" she asked.

"A candlelit bubble bath," he replied, darting into the bathroom to unload the candles. When he returned, he popped the champagne and they each took a glass.

"What shall we toast to?" she asked.

"To finding the one we love."

"To finding love."

They sipped their champagne and Finn said, "Shall we eat? I asked a chef to prepare salmon in caviar sauce."

During their succulent meal, they talked about the film, Ella's work, and their childhoods, and then Finn put the dinner tray in the hallway and scurried to set up the bath. Soon they were soaking in the tub, surrounded by the soft glow of candlelight. Ella leaned against Finn and sighed contentedly as he wrapped his strong arms around her.

"I thought about you all day today," he said.

"You did?"

"I couldn't get the image of you with those kids out of my head. You were such a natural with them."

"I'm crazy for tiny humans, always have been. I love their curiosity, big imaginations, big emotions. When a toddler is overjoyed, it's infectious. They can't contain it and it just oozes out of them. They feel everything so fully, so honestly, with their whole selves."

"Do you want to have children of your own?"

"Finn . . ."

He squeezed her waist and said, "Have you ever thought about it?"

"Have you?" she asked, turning to face him.

"Ella, I would love to have a family with you someday, when we're ready. Do you want to have a family with me?"

"Well, yes, but . . ."

"But what, baby?"

"I would want to have children *with* you, but I wouldn't want to have them *without* you."

"What do you mean?"

"The way I grew up, it just made me not want to do it on my own."

"You wouldn't be," he insisted. "We'd be together. I'm not going anywhere."

"Finn, there's more than one way to be alone. You spend your life flying around the world to shoot movies and attend film festivals. Where would that leave me? Alone."

"Sweetheart, if we choose to have a family someday, some things would obviously change. I've been thinking about this since we met, but I didn't want to bring it up and scare you away by asking too much too soon. But after I saw you today, I thought we could at least talk about it. It's just a conversation."

"You've been thinking about it all this time?"

"Yes," he said, gently running his fingers down her arm.

"What have you been thinking about?"

"Well, we could take some time to be alone together, to travel. If we had a child, you would both travel with me to film sets. I can get the studio to rent us a house. We'd hire a nanny and any other kind of help we want so you could write, I could work, and we could all be together. When our oldest is school-age, I would only take jobs in LA, except maybe in the summers when we could all still travel as a family. We could show them the world. Being a husband and father would be my priority. You wouldn't go to so much as a single doctor's appointment alone unless you wanted to. If I had to give up acting and be a stay-at-home dad, that's fine too."

"Wow. You've really thought about this."

"Well, yeah. I can't help it. Our future spilled out before me when you told me you love me. But it's just a fantasy. Sweetheart, there's no pressure. Until today, I didn't even know if children were a possibility. If we live our lives together, just the two of us, I'd be perfectly happy." He planted a soft kiss in her hair.

"Just a fantasy?" she asked.

"Yeah, for now. Do you ever fantasize about our future?"

She nodded.

"Tell me."

"Well, I always imagined that I'd keep working, but less than I do now. I'd want to spend time with my babies."

"Babies?" he asked. "How many?"

"Three. Two girls and then a boy. I don't care about gender, it's just what I imagine."

He rubbed her shoulder. "Tell me more."

"They'd all look like you," she said.

"Oh, see in my mind, each one of them looks just like you."

She smiled and he kissed the tip of her nose.

"Keep going," he said.

"Well, I like your idea of traveling together. I imagined that . . ."

"What, baby?"

"It's silly," she said.

"Tell me anyway."

"Well, it's just a fantasy, but I can picture us buying a little house in the French countryside for summers and holidays. You know, one of those old stone houses with wooden beams on the ceilings and a wood-burning stove, with plenty of room outside for the kids to roll around in the grass and a space for me to write." She crinkled her nose and shook her head. "I told you, it's silly."

"Not to me. I think it sounds perfect," he said, kissing her. "So, two girls and a boy, huh? I should warn you, I've always liked traditional names, like Emily and Sarah. I'm guessing you gravitate toward more free-spirited names like Lula Belle or Blue Moon. I'm prepared to fight you on this." He playfully put up his dukes, but she grabbed one of his hands and kissed it.

She laughed. "Actually, I was thinking if we had a girl, maybe we'd call her Betty. It's completely traditional but modern too. I don't know. It's just a thought."

"Betty, huh? I love it. And you know what else? I love you." He stopped to stroke the side of her face. "I love you so much, Ella. There's no fantasy we can't make a reality if we choose to. Come on, sweetheart. Let's dry off and slip into bed. I want to show you exactly how I feel about you."

CHAPTER 15

The evening before the final day of shooting, everyone clambered into the dining room to find Ella and Albie playing a tune together at the piano.

"We got here early, so we were just stealing a little musical moment," Albie explained.

"That's right," Ella said, putting her arm around him.

"Don't let us stop you," Jean said. "Play us something, like you did that time in Barcelona."

Everyone took their seats, and the waiter promptly served their usual drinks.

Ella smiled at Albie. "Shall we? How about our old standby?"

Albie chuckled. "Let's do it."

The others sipped their cocktails as the duo played The Beatles' "In My Life," giggling at each other the whole time. They finished to a standing ovation. Albie hugged Ella tightly. "Thank you," he whispered, and they joined their friends.

"That was great, sweetheart," Finn said as Ella plopped down beside him. "I have a gorgeous piano in my house, but I don't think it's ever been played. The decorator suggested it. Now I finally know its purpose."

She smiled. "I've always wanted a piano. Never had one. I don't get many opportunities to play, but I never miss a chance with Albie. One of his many talents."

"Life is a whole lot simpler sitting behind the eighty-eight," Albie said. "Ella and I love playing that song. Though I must say, it's become a bit more sentimental for me these days." He picked up his bourbon and slowly took a sip.

Ella looked at him and smiled warmly. "Go on," she said.

Albie nodded. "There's something I want to tell you all." He paused and took a breath before continuing. "Tomorrow's shoot will be my last."

"Are you retiring?" Charlotte asked.

"From life, I'm afraid," he replied.

The mood in the room instantly turned serious.

Jean asked, "The cancer? It's back?"

Albie nodded.

"Oh, Albie. I'm so sorry, old friend," Jean said.

"I don't know what to say. I'm terribly sorry," Finn said.

Everyone echoed these sentiments, but Albie interrupted. "Now let's have none of this. I'm an old man. I've lived my life. Damn well too."

They all feigned smiles.

"Tomorrow is the last day of shooting, and I didn't want to tell you at the wrap party and ruin everyone's fun, but I thought you should know."

Finn looked at him earnestly. "Albie, I want you to know that working with you has been one of the greatest experiences of my life. It's truly been an honor. I'll carry it with me always. And it hasn't just been about the acting—I've learned so much from you about love and passion for life."

"Likewise," Charlotte said, putting her hand on his shoulder. "You and I go way back. I've learned more from you over the years than you may realize. You're an extraordinary actor. Working with you has been such a gift. So has your friendship."

"The same for me," he replied, patting her hand.

"Albie, I'm stunned," Michael said. "You're larger than life, on and off screen. Truthfully, I never imagined that I'd get to work with an actor of your caliber. Like Finn said, it's been an honor, and it's been a blast getting to spend this time together. I just never expected that you'd be able to drink me under the table any night of the week."

Albie chuckled.

Willow began crying softly. "I'm sorry," she said. "I'm just so heartbroken. You've all become like family to me. Albie, working with you has changed my life. I never thought I'd have an opportunity like this. No one's ever taken me seriously before."

He smiled. "You're a fine actress. Extraordinary, really. Jean was right to cast you. You'll be the toast of Tinseltown when people see your performance. Make good choices, artistic choices, and the world will be your oyster. And don't take shit from anyone, you hear me?"

"Thank you," she murmured through laughter-laced tears.

Albie continued, "Okay, that's enough. I don't want to end this wonderful journey we've shared with sadness or pity. Frankly, I hate that shit."

They laughed.

"I want you all to know what a special project this has been for me. Couldn't think of a finer group to share my final curtain call with. Truly, I mean that." He raised his glass. "Here's to all of you and this little film of ours that asks the big questions."

They all raised their glasses and said, "Cheers."

Albie took a swig of his drink and looked at the faces of each of his beloved friends. "Thank you," he said. "Truly, thank you."

ELLA BRUSHED HER TEETH AND STOOD in the bathroom doorway, gazing absentmindedly at Finn.

"Hey, come here," he said, turning down the blanket on her side of the bed. She slipped into bed and burrowed into his chest. "I just can't believe it about Albie."

"I know," she replied.

"He's been at the top of his game this whole time. None of us had any idea."

"He really wanted to make one final film. It's been a good distraction for him. He's quite an actor, though; despite how it may have seemed, he's been in a lot of discomfort. That's why he's been drinking at night."

"I hope he makes it to see the film premiere."

"Me too. But honestly, I don't think it matters to him. He got what he needed from this experience. Besides, his imagination is so big, I'm sure he can envision the final film," she said.

"How long have you known?"

"A while. Couple months, I guess. Since right after you and I . . ."

He kissed her forehead.

"I'm sorry I couldn't tell you. He wanted to keep it private."

"I understand. Now I know why you've been spending so much time with him. You two are so sweet together." He ran his fingers down her arm and added, "After the way he spoke about his wife, I'm surprised he didn't want to spend this time with her."

"He didn't want to sit at home, waiting to die. Instead, he wanted to stay busy and make a special piece of art that would live on after he's gone. When we all leave the day after tomorrow, he'll head back to London. He plans to spend every last minute with Margaret. Said he'll pass on in her arms."

He squeezed her tightly. "Speaking of leaving, I know you didn't want to worry about it until we had to, and I've tried to be very good about not bringing it up, but we leave the day after tomorrow. I want to plan our life together. Have you thought more about coming to LA with me?"

"I need to fly to Paris. Jean can take me on his jet. I . . ."

"That's okay, sweetheart. Maybe you could go to your place first and then meet me in LA. I'll take care of the arrangements. I can send my jet or book you a flight, whatever you prefer. What do you think?"

Her body tensed, and she stared at her hands in her lap. "Could we wait until after the wrap party tomorrow night to talk about this? It doesn't make a difference right now, does it?"

Smiling softly, he stroked the side of her face. "Okay, baby." He nibbled on her earlobe and whispered, "I know how we can use this time."

LATE THE NEXT AFTERNOON, JEAN hollered, "Cut! That's a wrap!" The room exploded with cheers and applause. "Thank you to the entire cast and crew for a superb job. I think we have something special here. I'd like to call each of the lead actors up to take a bow," he said. "Michael Hennesey!"

Michael trotted to the center of the room as the cast and crew roared.

"Charlotte Reed!" Jean called, and she stepped beside Michael to more applause.

"Finn Forrester!" he yelled. As Finn joined the others, Ella jumped out of her seat, hooting and hollering. He smiled at her, blushing.

"Willow Barnes!" She confidently joined the others to rousing applause.

"And last but never least, the one, the only, the incomparable Albie Hughes!"

Albie sauntered up to deafening applause. Everyone began stomping their feet as they clapped and screamed, "Bravo! Bravo!" The other actors turned to Albie, bowed their heads in respect, and joined the chorus of applause. Then all five actors held hands and took a final bow.

"Everyone, we've been laboring on *Celebration* for months. Now it's finally time to celebrate what we've accomplished. Go change into your street clothes and meet us in the grand salon for a big blowout bash!" Jean announced. "I'm finally ready to relax, at least until I sit down to edit the damn thing. Plan to eat, drink, and dance until the wee hours."

Albie turned to his castmates and said, "That was quite a curtain call. Thank you, my fellow actors, my friends."

They all hugged one another, and Finn ran over and grabbed Ella. He picked her up and twirled her around in the air. He put her down and kissed her passionately, both dizzy from delight and desire. "We did it," he said. "The most unforgettable shoot of my life, in every way, done."

"You were amazing from start to finish. It's going to be a magnificent film."

"I'm going to dash over to my trailer to change. I'll meet you at the party. Save me a glass of bubbly."

"Will you dance with me?" she asked.

"All night."

CHAPTER 16

When Finn and Ella returned to the inn, they stopped at the front desk to request a morning wake-up call and then ambled to Ella's room, hand in hand.

"What an incredible experience this has been. It's hard to believe it's ending," Finn said. "I'm really going to miss everyone. This has been so different than any other film I've done. We became like a family."

"Yeah, Jean's projects are always special."

"Sweetheart, I know you didn't want to make plans in advance, but now we really need to figure things out. Are you sure you can't come to LA with me in the morning? I was hoping you'd move in with me like we talked about. We could send for your things."

She dropped his hand, walked over to the chair in the corner of the room, and sat down. She gazed despondently at her feet. In a faint voice, she muttered, "Finn, I can't do that. I . . ."

"That's okay, baby," he said, rushing over and kneeling in front of her. He took her hand. "My next project films in LA, and it doesn't start for about a month. After I fly back to LA to end things with Savannah, I could meet you in Paris. I know your place is small, but that just means we'll be cozy. We've spent so much time together in this room, and it's been perfect. We could spend a month at your place, and then you could come to LA with me for a few months." He massaged her hand and continued, "Or we could just use Paris as a starting point and take a vacation. Maybe the Amalfi Coast to reminisce about our first dance together. After that, who knows? We can figure it out. If you decide you like it in LA, you could move in with me then. Or maybe we'll go back and forth between LA and Paris. I really don't care where we make our home base as long as we're together. Hell, I'm willing to roam around with you like a vagabond if that's what you want. We can build any life we choose."

She took a deep breath and finally raised her gaze to meet his. "Finn, go back to your life. Go back to LA and be with Savannah."

"What are you talking about?" he asked, a look of shock sweeping across his face.

"It's okay," she said. "What happens on set, stays on set."

"Baby, no. It isn't like that. It never has been."

"I know how these things happen. Ours is hardly the first affair to occur on an exotic filming location. People are away from their lovers, maybe lonely, creating passionate art. Feelings become intensified." She paused. "This place is not real life, not even for you. It's like sleepaway camp when you're a kid—you bond with everyone and think it will always be that way, but then you go home to your normal life and they quickly fade from memory. You'll go back to LA, see Savannah, and slip right back into the life you left behind. Before you know it, I'll just be some woman you spent two months with once upon a time."

"I can't believe you're saying this. You will never be just some woman. Never." He stroked her cheek and took her hand in his. "Baby, you're the love of my life. I'm completely head over heels in love with you. It was true yesterday, it's true today, and it will be true tomorrow."

"I'm sure you'll feel differently when you see Savannah. The whole time we've been together, she has thought you're still with her. Maybe you wanted it that way, to keep your options open."

"Ella, I don't want Savannah. It was over before I even arrived here. The only reason I haven't ended it with her is because *you* told me to wait until I got back to California. My God, did you do that because you wanted an out?" he said, springing up and gripping his head in his hands. "Did you plan to leave me from the start?"

"I'm not leaving you, Finn. You were never mine, not really."

"How can you say that?" he asked, frantically pacing around the room they had shared, hurt and anger in his voice. "We talked about building a life together, having a family. We named our first daughter Betty as if we could both already see her."

"That was just a fantasy," she mumbled.

"Really? Is that all it was to you?" He paused and added, "It was real to me, and I think it was just as real to you. Don't you love me?"

"Please, I don't want this to be any harder than it has to be. Let's just cherish the memories of what we had. By this time tomorrow, you'll be back with Savannah. Or if you really do end things with her, you'll be with the next one in no time. You're an A-list movie star. You can have any woman you want."

"Apparently not. Ella, you're the only woman I want." He furrowed his brow. "My God, how could you think I could ever be with Savannah or anyone else after you? After what we've shared? You keep trying to tell me how I feel and what I'll do, but you're not listening to me. I don't want

Savannah. I don't want anyone else. I want *you*. I love *you*. Only you, always you, for the rest of my life." She didn't respond and didn't even look at him, so he started walking to the door. He put his hand on the knob, stopped, and turned to face her. "You're scared," he said softly. "You're scared, so you're trying to push me away."

She looked at him, tears in her eyes. He crossed the room and knelt before her, wiping away the tears sliding down her cheeks. "You've helped everyone here confront their fears and own their choices: Albie, Michael, Willow, Charlotte, and even me. But what about you, Ella? What about you?"

She sniffled and said, "Finn . . ."

"Sweetheart, after we made love for the first time, I asked you to tell me you were mine. It's because I was always afraid this would happen. I was afraid that what Jean said was true: you're unattainable. I tried to ease my insecurity the wrong way. Instead of asking you to say you're mine, I should have told you *I'm yours*. That's what you needed to know. I see that now. Baby, I'm yours, forever and always. Trust what we have. It's once in a lifetime."

She gently ran her finger across his lips. He smiled and whispered, "I love you. Do you love me?"

"Yes," she whispered. "I love you so much."

He pressed his forehead to hers. "I'm yours," he whispered. "I don't want to own you or change you or hurt you. All I want in this world is to love you." He pulled back, cupped her face in his hands, and pressed his mouth to hers. They began kissing softly and with increasing passion, running their fingers through each other's hair and pulling off their clothes. They stumbled onto the bed and made love tenderly, each whispering, "I love you," over and over again.

After making love, Finn wrapped Ella in his arms, continuing to gently kiss her. "What we have is so beautiful.

You can trust it. It's not a lie or a trick or a fantasy. It's not going to evaporate or be stolen away," he whispered. "I'm yours. I love you more than I could say. I always will."

"I love you too. Body and soul," she said.

He kissed her again. "Just sleep like this, curled up in my arms. When we're holding each other, it's easy to remember that we belong together. We can figure out the details in the morning. Okay, baby?"

She nodded. "Don't let go," she said, closing her eyes.

THE NEXT MORNING, THE PHONE RANG at the crack of dawn. Finn leaned over and answered the wake-up call. When he put the receiver down, he rolled over and found that Ella wasn't in bed. He stretched his arms and sat up. Ella was balled up in the chair in the corner of the room, chain-smoking.

"Hey," he said.

"Hey," she muttered.

He got up, put on his underwear and pants, and walked over to Ella. She was distant, so he knelt on the floor before her and laid his head on her lap.

"I promised Jean I'd go to the Cannes Film Festival for the premiere. I'll see you there," she said.

He popped his head up, trying to read her face. "Cannes? That's in May. It's seven months away," he replied. "Baby, what are you doing?"

"Just go and live your life, Finn. If you'll always love me, then when we see each other at Cannes, we'll choose to be together." She paused and said, "But you and I both know that when we meet on that red carpet, I'll just be some woman you once spent a couple of months with. You'll give me an awkward little hug or a peck on the cheek, make some small talk, and go about your life without giving it a second thought. Maybe you'll even be relieved you didn't throw your life away for a brief affair."

He looked down, ran his hand through his hair, and muttered, "I can't believe you're doing this." He raised his gaze to meet hers. "This isn't what you really want. I know you, baby. You're going to regret this. I can see it in your eyes—you already do. It's why you got out of bed and sat over here. If you were in my arms, if we were touching, you could never say these things to me. We love each other too much. You love me, I know you do. You're just not convinced of my love for you. I want to prove my love every day for the rest of my life." He reached out and traced the outline of her fingers. She inhaled and he said, "You're just scared."

"Please, Finn. Don't make it harder."

"The first night we spent together, you said, 'Don't ever go.' You meant it. Sweetheart, I don't want to leave you."

"Please, Finn. I'll see you in Cannes in the spring."

He sighed heavily before rising. He grabbed his shirt and shoes off the floor and turned to face her. "Ella, a relationship is two people being courageous together. I can't do it for you. Please, trust what we have and take the leap with me."

She just stared at him with a haze of sadness in her eyes. He turned and walked out the door, closing it gently behind him.

A COUPLE OF HOURS LATER, the driver was ready to ferry the five actors on the long ride to the airport. Michael, Willow, and Charlotte had said their goodbyes and were waiting in the van. Albie thanked Jean and then hugged Ella tightly. "Take it from an old bugger like me: life is short. Love is what matters. You two are in love. Don't blow it, kid," he whispered. She squeezed him tighter and he said, "I'm going to spend every last minute I have with my beloved Margaret. I'll be in her arms when I take my final breath. Don't let fear ruin your shot at real love and happiness. That's all that matters. Love, Ella. *Love*."

When they parted, she said, "I'll be thinking of you. Please be well. I hope to see you in Cannes."

Albie smiled. "I fear I won't make it to see our project up on the silver screen. I do hope our special little film that asks the big questions will inspire people to grab life with gusto. Perhaps it will even inspire you." He winked, kissed the top of her head, and then climbed into the van.

Finn stood in the doorway, looking down. "Thank you again," he said to Jean, shaking his hand. Then he turned to Ella, kissed her politely on her cheek, and muttered, "Goodbye," without looking in her eyes. With that, he left.

Ella gasped, collapsed onto Jean's chest, and burst into tears. He rubbed her back as she sobbed uncontrollably. He whispered, "*Ma chérie*, you are in love with him."

"Yes," she mumbled through her cries.

"Why did you do this thing?" he asked.

"I don't know."

 CHAPTER 17

Ella shuffled into her apartment and dropped her luggage by the door. Her flat felt stuffy and smelled stale after three months of vacancy, so she opened the balcony doors and allowed a fresh breeze to blow through the small space. She inhaled deeply and tried to catch her breath, but her gaze was drawn to her keepsake chest. She flipped the top open, rifled around, and pulled out her old teddy bear, the white silk ribbon around its neck discolored and frayed. As she held it, tears exploded from her eyes. Clutching the teddy bear, she crawled into bed and cried herself to sleep.

"DARLING, IS THAT YOU?" Margaret called as Albie walked through the door.

"Yes, my love. I'm home."

She hurried over and they hugged tightly. Albie put his hand on her cheek, and they looked into each other's eyes. "Is it possible you got even more beautiful?" he asked.

She smiled. "Older, yes. More beautiful? Doubtful. Perhaps your eyesight has worsened."

"You would be wrong, but there's a first time for everything."

She blushed and they kissed softly. "Oh, how I missed that," he whispered.

"Me too," she said. "How are you feeling, darling? I've been worried about you."

"Life is too short to waste time worrying. I'm so glad to be back home with you."

"I thought you might be hungry. Lunch is ready. I made a ham and cheese quiche and a green salad so I can get something healthy in you. Can only imagine all the trash you've eaten these last three months. Come sit with me; you can tell me all about the film."

Albie chuckled. "I truly did miss you, my love."

"Yes, yes, come along then."

They sat beside each other at the dining room table. Margaret poured their tea and served Albie a slice of quiche with a heaping side of salad.

Albie smiled and took a bite of savory quiche. "The food at the inn was quite good, but nothing compares to your cooking. Seems every time you make me something in a pie crust, I fall in love with you a little more."

Margaret chuckled. "How did the shoot go?"

"Best film I've ever been in, hands down. Jean really went for it. I believe it's the kind of film that will stick with people and push them to reflect on the big questions in their own lives."

"I had reservations, but I'm so glad you did it, although I missed you terribly. What a wonderful project. From our phone calls, it sounds like you had quite a lovely time with everyone."

"I did. Splendid group of actors. It was great fun breaking bread with them every day. Perhaps I even taught them a few things."

"You're a gifted actor," Margaret said. "I'm sure they all learned a great deal from working with you."

He shook his head. "That's not what I mean. Let's just say that they were each dealing with some personal issues. You know young people, thinking they have all the time in the world. Sometimes they lose track of what matters most, can't tell their ass from their elbow."

"Yes, well, our bodies might be slowly decomposing, but at least we've always had the sense to follow our hearts," she said.

"Ella did something damn foolish."

"She's always been such a lovely girl."

"She still is, but foolish nonetheless," Albie replied.

"You told me she fell in love with Finn Forrester."

"That's right, deeply in love, but she didn't trust it. Got scared, I suppose. Fucked it all up."

"Perhaps she can still make it right."

He smiled warmly. "On the flight home, I could only think about you, about how I couldn't wait to see you, and about how blessed we've been. It's such a gift to feel so comfortable with someone that you always want them around because somehow they make things immeasurably better." He picked up her hand and kissed it softly. "Let's spend every moment together. I'll even help you in the garden, my black thumb and all. I know I'll drive you mad, so I'll try my best to behave."

She giggled.

"Really, my love, the only thing I want is to be with you."

CHARLOTTE WALKED OUT OF HER bathroom in her robe. She was towel-drying her hair when she heard her husband come through the front door of their flat.

"Charlotte, I'm home."

She met him in the living room. "Hi."

"Sorry I couldn't be here when you got back. We had a matinee performance," he said, giving her a peck on the lips.

"How'd it go?" she asked.

"Good. It was a full house. The lighting crew fouled something up in the second act, but it's doubtful anyone noticed. Tell me, what was it like working with Jean? I know you had a rough go in the beginning, but it sounded like things sorted themselves out. Was it everything you hoped?"

"Yes, it was extraordinary, but . . ."

"Don't take it personally. His temper is legendary. I've heard some actors—"

"I want to have a child," she blurted out. "I'm sorry. I didn't mean to say it that way, but I fear I'll lose my courage."

"Charlotte . . ."

"Yes, yes, I know. It's not a good time to talk about it. There will never be a good time. Is it that you don't want to have a child? Or is it me? Us? Perhaps you don't want to have a family with me."

"Love, is that really what you think?" he asked, rubbing her shoulders.

She glanced down. "I . . . I don't know."

"Charlotte, I love you. When we married, you told me how important your career was to you, that it was the most important thing in your life. I promised you we would live as artists. The last thing I want is for you to give any part of that up and then resent me for it."

"I wouldn't, ever. Fifteen years ago, acting was all I could think about. There was so much I had yet to discover about my art form, and through it, about myself. My dreams are different now. I want a family. Maybe I wouldn't be a good mother. Perhaps that's your concern, and . . ."

"Charlotte, no. You'd be an extraordinary mother," he said, caressing her cheek. "I looked through the information you found on adoption."

"You did?"

He nodded. "I didn't say anything while you were away because I didn't want to distract you and I really thought you'd be too high on acting again when you returned."

"The whole time I was gone, I fantasized about us having a baby. I stopped taking my birth control pills when I was away, just in case. I planned to go back on them if you didn't agree. Can we try the old-fashioned way and see what happens? If we don't have any luck, we can explore alternatives."

"I have a couple of hours before I need to get back to the theater. There's no time like the present."

She untied her sash and let her robe fall to the floor.

"PUT THE BAGS THERE," MICHAEL directed his driver. He slipped him a tip and locked the door behind him. He looked around the empty apartment, filled with leather furniture, modern appliances, and deafening silence. He meandered into the kitchen, where his staff had left a meal in the refrigerator. As his dinner was warming up in the microwave, he listened to his voicemail. There were a dozen messages from women, each offering to come over, one offering to welcome him home with nothing but a G-string and a can of whipped cream. He grabbed his phone, trying to decide who to call, but he ended up dialing Lauren's number.

"Hello?" she said.

"Hey, Lauren. It's me, Michael."

"Oh, hi. It's kind of late."

"Sorry about that. I just got back from filming in Europe."

"Sophie's asleep."

"Yeah, I figured she would be. How's she doing?"

"Fine."

"Did she like the art camp?" he asked.

"Loved it. I fear she may want to follow in your footsteps. Thanks for sending the money."

"Listen, I was hoping to make plans to see her."

"She's got school every day."

"Maybe I could pick her up after school one day."

"Michael," she started, "I really don't think sending your assistant to pick her up at school is the best thing for her."

"I wouldn't send anyone. I'd go myself. Maybe we could go for ice cream or something. Or maybe I could take her out somewhere next weekend. She's never slept over at my place, so maybe . . ."

"You can't waltz in and out of her life when it suits you. It's too confusing for her."

He sighed. "That's fair, but it's not what I mean. I'd like to be a real part of her life. I realize you have every reason to be cautious and angry, but she's my daughter. Please, Lauren. I'll do it however you want until I can earn your trust and hers."

There was a long silence, and eventually Lauren said, "You can take her out to dinner tomorrow night. But Michael, if you screw this up . . ."

"I won't. I promise."

"Come by at five o'clock. She'll be ready."

"Would you like to join us? We can go anywhere you want. Maybe Thai food? I know it's your favorite."

"Michael . . ."

"I miss you. I miss you more than I can say. If you're not seeing anyone, I thought maybe . . ."

"You can't do this to me. Or to Sophie."

"Please, Lauren. No matter what happens, I promise I'll be there for Sophie. Not just checks in the mail, I'll really be there. But if there's any way you might also give me another chance . . ."

"After the way you treated me . . ."

"I know," he said, wincing. "I was a total fuckup, which

I regret more than you'll ever know. I've regretted it all these years and have been too cowardly to make it right. I'm so sorry. Please, just one dinner, the three of us. That's all I'm asking for."

"We'll see you at five. Good night."

"Good night."

"JEEZ, THAT WAS SUCH A LONG FLIGHT. I'm exhausted," Willow said as Brian jumped in the back of the SUV beside her.

"You'll have a couple of days off before you're scheduled to work," he replied.

"What are you talking about? I didn't think I had anything booked."

"Remember, that music video I told you about? Don't worry, it'll be a two-day shoot max, right on a soundstage in LA. Easy. Then next week is the *Maxim* cover shoot."

"Brian, I told you I didn't know if I wanted to take those jobs."

"I know, I know. I just figured it was nerves before you left for Sweden."

"Brian . . ."

"Look, if you're really too wiped, I can see about pushing the magazine shoot."

"It's not that. It's just . . ."

"Trust me, you'll be glad for the exposure. This is your big comeback," he explained. "You need to make a splash and strike while the iron is hot. You're getting older. I don't know how much longer we can capitalize on your looks."

She turned to face him with steely eyes. "You know, not that you asked, but I was actually pretty good in the film. Everyone said so. Being part of something artistic like that, well, it helped me reconnect with why I started in entertainment in the first place."

"That's great, doll. I haven't wanted to push you, but there's a lot of interest rolling in. I can book you for a million things. There's one promising script that came in—you'd play a drug-addicted stripper. It's not a big role, but it's . . ."

"Brian, that's not what I want. None of it is," she said forcefully.

"Doll . . ."

"I'm speaking. Please let me finish. I realize you've looked out for me for a long time, so it's been difficult for me to say this, but you work for me. I don't work for you. We have completely different visions for my career. No more men's magazines and stripper roles. I want to make notable films. I was even thinking about doing live theater; it would be such a great learning experience. Not all actors can sing and dance like I can. I want to take acting classes to work on my craft, to get better."

"There's no reason to waste your time . . ."

"You're not listening to me."

"Willow, doll, if the classes are important to you . . ." he started.

"Brian, this isn't working anymore. I'm going to be looking for a new management team, effective immediately. I want to work with people who take me seriously."

"Doll . . ."

"There's nothing left to say. Cancel anything you've booked for me, and make it clear that you never had my approval."

He snorted. "Just because you landed one Jean Mercier film doesn't mean you can suddenly parlay that into a career as a serious actress. You're no Charlotte Reed. Staying on brand is in your best interest."

"Willow Barnes isn't a brand, she's a person, she's me. I'm not a child anymore. From now on, I'll decide what's in my best interest." She paused and added, "You're right,

I'm not Charlotte Reed, but I held my own with her and I hope to be just as good as she is someday. I've made mistakes, but I've learned from them. Maybe you're right and I'll never land the kind of roles I dream about, but I owe it to the little girl I was who dreamt of being a real performer to at least try."

"Listen . . ."

"Someone who doesn't see me as a serious actress is never going to be able to help make my dream a reality, so there's nothing left to say." She rolled down her window, breathing in the warm LA air, which suddenly felt anew with possibility.

"BABE, YOU'RE BACK!" SAVANNAH exclaimed as she jumped into Finn's arms.

"What are you doing here?" he asked.

"I relieved your house sitter a couple of hours ago. Come into the kitchen. I ordered Chinese food for a late-night dinner."

"Savannah, we need to talk."

"Finn, just come have something to eat and then . . ."

"What I have to say can't wait."

She rubbed his biceps and said, "It's okay. Your dalliance with the makeup girl or whoever went a little further than we agreed to. I get it. I forgive you, babe. Now come and . . ."

"No, we need to talk. Now."

THE NEXT DAY AT NOON, ELLA FINALLY crawled out of bed, her eyes swollen and bloodshot. She grabbed her phone and listened to her voicemail. There was a message from Jean.

"*Ma chérie*, I'm calling to check on you. My guess is you cried yourself to sleep last night. You have a choice,

Ella. You can try to go about your life as if nothing ever happened, or you can figure out why you pushed him away. Take it from someone who has fucked up every relationship I've been in: I've never loved anyone the way you and Finn love each other. It's not too late. You'll never have the happiness you deserve unless you're brave. Be brave, *ma chérie*, in your life as you are in your work. Ask yourself the big questions. He's worth it. So are you."

After deleting the message, she opened a text from Willow to see the photograph they had all taken together. When she saw herself sitting joyfully with Finn, his arm around her, she began to weep. "I do love him," she mumbled. "Be brave. Ask the big questions. Like why the fuck did I do that? Why was I so scared? Am I so afraid of being abandoned or hurt that I can't trust love will last?" She grabbed her laptop and plopped into bed, her teddy bear beside her. She took a deep breath, opened her browser, and ran a search for local therapists.

 CHAPTER 18

"The sun always shines brightly for the Cannes Film Festival," Jean said as they arrived at the Palais des Festivals et des Congrès. "Not a cloud in sight. It's another picture-perfect day in the French Riviera."

Ella smoothed the sides of her strapless black satin mermaid-style gown and touched the green amber hanging from her neck, on full display with her hair pulled back into a loose French braid. "You are stunning, *ma chérie*," he said, taking her hand. "Shall we?" he asked as they entered the iconic scene: the famous red carpet sprawling before them, hordes of entertainment reporters hollering and cameras flashing on both sides of the carpet, and fans eagerly trying to catch a glimpse of their favorite Hollywood stars. They met up with Michael and his date.

"Jean, Ella, great to see you both," he said. "This is Lauren."

"Pleased to meet you," Ella said, noticing the brown amber earrings dangling from her ears and matching bracelet around her wrist.

"Nice to meet you too," Lauren replied. "Michael has told me so much about you both and what a wonderful time he had making this film."

"He told us about you too," Ella said.

Lauren smiled shyly, tilting her head down. Michael put his hand on the small of her back and pecked her cheek, careful not to smudge her makeup.

"Our daughter is back at the hotel," he said. "We've made a family vacation out of it."

"I'm so happy for you," Ella said.

"Speaking of family, have you seen Charlotte?" Michael asked, gesturing down the carpet.

They turned and saw Charlotte in a flowing rose-colored gown, proudly showing off a baby bump.

"Oh my goodness!" Ella exclaimed.

"She's five and a half months pregnant," Michael said.

"That's fantastic. Are the others here?" Ella asked.

"Willow is halfway down the carpet, speaking with reporters. They're all dying to hear about her upcoming starring role on Broadway."

Jean smiled. "I always knew she was a real actress. Wait until you see the final cut of the film. She's going to be the darling of Tinseltown, just as Albie predicted. There will be a slew of award nominations in her future."

Ella smiled, her eyes darting around and scanning the crowd. She turned back to Michael and asked, "Finn? Is he here?"

Michael shook his head. "Not yet."

"Oh," Ella said, looking down.

Jean squeezed her hand. "He will be here, *ma chérie*. Come, the press is waiting." He took her hand and they walked slowly down the line of media, stopping along the way so Jean could answer questions about the film. Ella stood back, casually glancing down toward the entrance. They were halfway down the red carpet when she saw Finn arrive, looking more handsome than ever in a black tuxedo. He noticed her immediately and they made eye contact. He began making his way toward her, stopping several times to pose for obligatory photos. Before he reached her, the reporters began hollering for the stars of *Celebration* to pose together.

"I'll walk ahead a bit," Ella said to Jean. "Go do your thing. Celebrate this magnificent cinematic achievement."

Jean, Willow, Michael, Charlotte, and Finn joined each other in the middle of the carpet. They stopped to greet one another with hugs and handshakes before posing in a line to a flurry of flashbulbs. When the press gallery was satisfied, Jean, Willow, Michael, and Charlotte each walked over to different reporters for on-camera interviews. Finn made a beeline for Ella. She reciprocated, and they met in the center of the carpet.

They stood for a moment, staring deeply into each other's eyes, neither quite able to exhale.

"Uh, you look beautiful," Finn stammered, pecking her on the cheek.

"Thank you. I'm so happy to see you."

"You're wearing the necklace I bought you."

"Yes. Finn—"

He cut her off. "It's great to see everyone again. Seems like they're all doing well. You were right, Michael did make things right with Lauren. And now I see why Charlotte was so emotional during our big scene. Obviously, it worked out for her."

She smiled. "Yes, it's wonderful. I only wish Albie were here."

"I know. It's hard to believe he's gone. It was such an honor to work with him, to get to know him. I'm sorry he never got to see the final film."

"In his mind, I think he saw it," she said.

"I sent his wife flowers since there was no public memorial."

"I know," she said. "They were gorgeous."

He looked at her quizzically.

"I checked in on him after the shoot ended. When he was at home in hospice near the end, I visited him and Margaret. After he passed, I stayed for a few days to help."

"You did?" he asked.

She nodded. "He got his wish: he died in Margaret's arms. The day before he passed, he told me that he felt bad burdening her that way, leaving her with such loss, but he chose to look at it as a gift. The pain she would feel was in direct proportion to the lifetime of love they shared." She paused for a moment before continuing. "He was right. When he was gone, all she could do was talk about him and look at photos of their life together. Every tear was laced with love. Those memories brought her peace, even pleasure."

They stared at each other for a long, intimate moment, as if no one else were there. Finn finally broke the silence. "How have you been?"

"Not well. It's been really hard, being without you," she said softly as tears filled her eyes.

"Ella . . ."

"Please, Finn. I need to tell you how deeply sorry I am for what I did. I know I hurt you terribly, and I would do anything to take it back."

He took her hand and said, "The worst part was that, as devastated as I was, I knew you were hurting just as much and I couldn't help you."

"Finn, you were right. I was scared," she said, tears trickling down her cheeks.

He used his thumbs to gently wipe away her tears. "Ella . . ."

"Please, there are things I have to say to you. I realize you may be with someone else and that I've probably lost my chance, but I need you to know how profoundly sorry I am and how much I love you, how much I've always loved you. I love you simply because I can't help but to love you, and I don't need another reason." He inhaled sharply, ready to speak, but she continued. "When you left, I spent twenty-four hours crying hysterically. It was the most agonizing pain of my life. The next day, I got up and found a therapist."

"You did?" he asked.

She nodded. "I wanted to reach out to you so many times, but I knew it wasn't fair to you. I needed to deal with my own stuff first so I could be certain I'd never hurt you again." He smiled at her softly. "I even got a kitten. She's very sweet."

"A kitten?" he asked.

"I needed to know if I could take care of someone else."

His smile grew. "I like kittens. What's her name?"

"Sweden."

"Oh, Ella."

"There's not been a moment that's gone by that I haven't thought of you and wished I could turn back the clock. All I can say is that I was terrified, but I'm not anymore. The only thing I'm scared of is living my life without you. If you've moved on, well, I'll have to find a way to live with it. But Finn, if there's any part of you that wants to give me another chance, I love you. I love you body and soul, and I always will. I trust what we have with all my heart."

He took a breath, smiled widely, and knelt down on bended knee. Witnessing the scene, reporters scurried to get closer, igniting a frenzied storm of flashbulbs. Finn slipped a small velvet box out of his pocket and opened it, revealing a blinding oval diamond engagement ring on a sparkling band. "Ella Sinclair, you are the love of my life. Together, we can live an adventure of our own making. Will you marry me?"

Her eyes flooded. "Yes. Yes, I'll marry you," she gasped through her tears.

He slipped the ring on her finger, rose, and swept her off her feet, whirling her around in the air. The sound of cameras clicking and fans cheering was deafening. Their friends all turned and joined the chorus of enthusiastic applause. When he set her down, he cupped her cheeks and they kissed passionately.

"Oh, baby, I missed you so much," he whispered.

"I've never been so happy in all my life. Tell me it isn't a dream," she said.

"Sweetheart, when I got back to LA, Savannah was waiting for me. I broke up with her on the spot. I bought you that ring the very next day. I decided that whenever we saw each other again, if you had figured out what I always knew, that we belong together, I'd know you were ready for me to propose. After all, I promised you I would." He stroked the side of her face. "Baby, I haven't been with anyone else. I could never be. I was waiting for you."

She leaned forward and pressed her mouth to his, melting into his familiar embrace.

"So, where do we live?" he asked.

"I don't care where we live, only how we live: with nothing but love." They both smiled and she said, "I live where you live."

"And I live where you live," he said, kissing her softly again.

"The room you told me about in your house sounded nice, the one I could use for an office," she said.

He smiled. "I had that room cleared out a week after I got home from Sweden. Every day since, I've walked by that empty room, hoping one day you'd choose to fill it."

She put her hand on his cheek. "I'm going to love you so well, with everything I have. I promise I will never disappoint or hurt you again."

"I know, sweetheart."

"Oh, how I wish Albie were here. He'd be so happy to know how things turned out. We talked about something during our last conversation that I'm thinking of now."

"What's that?" he asked.

"He was so cross with me for screwing things up with you. Called me a fool. Made me promise I'd make it right. Told me he was dying and didn't have time for my bullshit, so I had better figure things out quickly."

Finn laughed. "Sounds like him."

"The day before he passed, Margaret went to make him a cup of tea. I was sitting on the edge of his bed, holding his hand. He talked about the film and how much he loved making it with all of you, that it was fitting for his final film to ask the big questions of life. Then he asked if I knew what the biggest question of all was. I shook my head and he said, 'Whether it is better to love or be loved.' Then he said, 'People foul that one up all the time because they're scared and insecure.' I asked him what he meant, and he said, 'You figure it out. Then you'll have everything you need to make it right.' He squeezed my hand and said, 'I'm tired now.' I left him to rest. That was the last time we spoke."

"Did you figure out what he meant?"

"Yes. It's not about being loved or looking to others to fill something within us. It's far better *to* love, because then you exist in a constant state of hope." She glanced down the carpet at Michael with his arm around Lauren, Willow confidently speaking with the press, and Charlotte rubbing her belly. She turned back to Finn and said, "That's what I want: to love you, to love you fearlessly with everything I have, and to allow you the same."

EPILOGUE

October 2   *Entertainment News Report*

The world witnessed their unforgettable, show-stopping engagement at the Cannes Film Festival, and now they've made it official. Yesterday, legendary actor Finn Forrester married writer Gabriella Sinclair at a star-studded bash held on the grounds of the estate the couple shares in Los Angeles. Celebrities in attendance included Jean Mercier, Michael Hennesey, Charlotte Reed, Willow Barnes, and Margaret Hughes, widow of the late actor Albie Hughes. The groom wore a classic black Gucci suit, and the bride stunned in a strapless white satin Vera Wang gown, her hair partially pulled back in a short veil. She carried a bouquet of colorful wildflowers tied with a white silk ribbon. Guests report it was a romantic affair and that the newlyweds couldn't take their eyes off each other as they danced to Elvis Presley's "Can't Help Falling in Love." Finn gifted his bride a chateau in the French countryside, which they plan to use as a holiday home. We're told the lucky guests were treated to an extravagant Swedish meal that ended with a five-tiered white wedding cake with layers of blueberry preserves. Rumor has it that the star and his bride are looking forward to a private honeymoon on the Amalfi Coast.

ACKNOWLEDGMENTS

Thank you to the entire team at She Writes Press, especially Brooke Warner and Shannon Green. I'm incredibly grateful for your unfailing support. I also extended a spirited thank-you to Crystal Patriarche at BookSparks for helping readers find this book. Thank you to the early reviewers for your generous endorsements. Sincere appreciation to Shalen Lowell, world-class assistant and spiritual bodyguard. Heartfelt thanks to Celine Boyle for your invaluable feedback. Thank you to Clear Voice Editing for the always phenomenal copyediting services. Liza Talusan and the Saturday Writing Team—thank you for building such a supportive community and allowing me to be a part of it. To my social media community and colleagues, thank you boundlessly for your support. My deep gratitude to my friends, especially Vanessa Alssid, Melissa Anyiwo, Pamela Martin, Sandra Faulkner, Ally Field, Jessica Smartt Gullion, Laurel Richardson, Xan Nowakowski, Mr. Barry Shuman, Eve Spangler, and J. E. Sumerau. As always, my love to my family. Madeline Leavy-Rosen, you are my light. Mark Robins, you're the best spouse in the world. Thank you for all that words cannot capture.

ABOUT THE AUTHOR

PATRICIA LEAVY, PhD, is a best-selling author. She has published over forty books, earning commercial and critical success in both nonfiction and fiction, and her work has been translated into numerous languages. Over the course of her career, she has also served as series creator and editor for ten book series, and she cofounded *Art/Research International: A Transdisciplinary Journal*. She has received over forty book awards. Recently, *Hollyland* received a 2022 Literary Titan Award for Fiction. She has also received career awards from the New England Sociological Association, the American Creativity Association, the American Educational Research Association, the International Congress of Qualitative Inquiry, and the National Art Education Association. In 2016, Mogul, a global women's empowerment network, named her an "Influencer." In 2018, the National Women's Hall of Fame honored her, and SUNY New Paltz established the "Patricia Leavy Award for Art and Social Justice." Please visit www.patricialeavy.com for more information.

Author photo © Mark Robins

SELECTED TITLES FROM SHE WRITES PRESS

She Writes Press is an independent publishing company founded to serve women writers everywhere. Visit us at www.shewritespress.com.

Hollyland by Patricia Leavy. $17.95, 978-1-64742-296-7. When writer and arts researcher Dee Schwartz meets famous actor Ryder Field outside a bar one night, the romance that blossoms seems like a fairy tale . . . until Dee disappears into thin air after an awards ceremony, making everyone wonder if the fairy tale will have a darker ending than anyone could have anticipated.

Chuckerman Makes a Movie by Francie Arenson Dickman. $16.95, 978-1-63152-485-1. New York City bachelor David Melman is a successful brander of celebrity fragrances. Laurel Sorenson, a leggy blonde, is a screenwriter on the brink of Hollywood success. When David, pushed by his bossy sister, agrees to take a screenwriting class taught by Laurel, an unlikely romance blooms—and that's just beginning of their troubles.

In the Heart of Texas by Ginger McKnight-Chavers. $16.95, 978-1-63152-159-1. After spicy, forty-something soap star Jo Randolph manages in twenty-four hours to burn all her bridges in Hollywood, along with her director/boyfriend's beach house, she spends a crazy summer back in her West Texas hometown—and it makes her question whether her life in the limelight is worth reclaiming.

Unreasonable Doubts by Reyna Marder Gentin. $16.95, 978-1-63152-413-4. Approaching thirty and questioning both her career path and her future with her long-time boyfriend, jaded New York City Public Defender Liana Cohen gets a new client—magnetic, articulate, earnest Danny Shea. When she finds herself slipping beyond the professional with him, she is forced to confront fundamental questions about truth, faith, and love.

Wishful Thinking by Kamy Wicoff. $16.95, 978-1-63152-976-4. A divorced mother of two gets an app on her phone that lets her be in more than one place at the same time, and quickly goes from zero to hero in her personal and professional life—but at what cost?